THE ENTITY'S WAR

A SHAWN CRAWFORD
ADVENTURE

THE ENTITY'S WAR

A SHAWN CRAWFORD
ADVENTURE

BY

TIM O'LEARY

OTHER SHAWN CRAWFORD ADVENTURES

BY TIM O'LEARY

The Gateway

Time Dimensions

The Dimensional Gateway

The Assigner

Missions

Nathan

Christopher

The Narragansett Trail: A Horror Story

Emily: A Horror Story

The Cradle of evil: A Horror Story

Tim O'Hara: The Early Years

The O'Hara Brothers: The Professional Years

LT. Tim O'Hara, United States Navy

Sancha

Warriors

Knights

Nowhere To Run: A Story of Maternal Abuse

The Ethereal Presence: A Time Travel Adventure

Joey

Kennebunk: A Horror Story

The Last War

Aruba

The Portal

The Entity

The Entity's Child

The Entity's Chosen

CDR J. Hunter King

Saving Kuwait: A Soldier's Memoir

A Demon Tetrology

For

My Son-in-Law, Duane Coffill, an excellent horror writer, who assisted in putting this book together, thank you.

For

His lovely Wife Shelley, may she always show empathy and a willing loving heart.

For

My Grandchildren, Maddie and Savannah, may they always show the kindness to others and the love for one another.

FOREWORD

The Entity has been a common character thread throughout all of my Shawn Crawford Books. An Intergalactic Being who protects the Good against all Evil, The Entity intervenes against injustices in the world. He uses Sir Shawn Crawford as His Agent to circumvent time through His Gateway. Crawford is the epitome of a Warrior who truly cares about the well-being of all.

Crawford's Seventh Degree Black Belt prowess in the Art of Wing Tsung, his training in the Art of Silent Killing and his being a fierce Advocate for the rights of the down-trodden make him the ideal intervention force to complete missions for The Entity. Shawn speaks eight languages fluently and holds two Doctoral Degrees. His United States Military Service defines him as mission-oriented. Crawford is the consummate Pilot in that he is qualified in OH-58D Kiowa Warrior, AH-1G Cobra Gunship, F-22B Raptor, F-42A Tiger Shark and F-193B Leopard Advanced Stealth Fighter Aircraft. And his experience as a Delta Force Operator in Syria truly complements his ability to adapt and overcome any posing threat to himself, his Family, and to his home base, Sydney, Australia in the year 2074.

This book is a story about how Nations seek ultimate Regional and World power through force. This is also a saga of opposing sides fiercely fighting for the freedom to live, to choose, and to celebrate for what has been given to them. Enjoy the Moment!

CAST OF CHARACTERS

FIRST LIEUTENANT WILL CARUSO: Royal Australian Plane Captain to the F-42A Tiger Shark and B-193B Advanced Fighter Aircraft. Highly intelligent, irreverent and carefree spirit and Crew Chief with a meticulous eye problem- solving regarding all Fixed-Wing and Rotary-Wing Aircraft in the Defense inventory. Awarded the Meritorious Service Medal for his accomplishments in aircraft fighter support to the Royal Australian Air Force. Member of The Entity's Inner Circle. Time era origination: 2074.

STAFF SERGEANT MADELYN

COFFILL: Royal Australian Air Force, Chief Administrative Assistant 'Gatekeeper' for Marshal Allison Morrison. Very efficient in the performance of her duties while displaying an intemperate exterior but harboring a heart of gold and boundless inner kindness. Chief Guardian to Colette Roberts-Crawford in the absence of Lady Christine Roberts. Time era origination: 2074.

SIR STEVEN SHAWN CRAWFORD: Air Marshal, Royal Australian Air Force, former Lieutenant Colonel, United States Army, Husband to Lady Christine Roberts, Father to Christopher and Colette, Pilot, OH-58D Kiowa Warrior, AH-1G Cobra Gunship and RAH-66 Comanche Attack Helicopters. The F-42A Tiger Shark and F-193B Leopard Advanced Stealth Fighter Aircraft. Moral, modest, and irreverent contributor to every major of personnel involvement. Chief expert in the understanding of Gateway/Wormhole events. Principal deterrent to the assassination attempts on the lives of various historical figures. Audacious and fierce devotee toward protecting the rights of those oppressed. Twice awarded the United States Medal of Honor, a Hero in the Third World War, Seventh Degree Black Belt Martial Arts Specialist and Expert in the art of Silent Killing. Speaks eight foreign languages and former Delta Force Black

Ops Member. Triple Ace against enemy Air Force Aggressors in aerial combat. Holds a Doctorate Degree in Advanced Aeronautical Engineering and Quantum Mechanics with Degrees in Economics and Chemistry from Georgia Southern University. Member of the Australian Government's Intelligence Agency. Never misses a good Beef Wellington dinner. Favorite of The Entity. Time era origination: 2017.

CHRISTINE ROBERTS CRAWFORD: The temporal Mother of Christopher and Colette Roberts-Crawford. Wife of Shawn Crawford. F-22 Raptor Pilot who recorded more than 15 aerial 'kills' while flying against German Nazi Aircraft during a time

travel sojourn. Given the Title of 'Lady'
Christine for her role in saving the
Australian Ambassador in the year
2074. Proficient in flying both the F-
42A Tiger Shark as well as the F-193B
Leopard Advanced Stealth Fighter
Aircraft. An Agent of The Entity. Time
era origination: 2017.

**CHRISTOPHER ROBERTS-
CRAWFORD:** The temporal Son of
Shawn and Christine. Seventh Degree
Black Belt Martial Arts Specialist.
Speaks eight foreign languages. An
advanced Fighter Pilot with more than
10 aerial 'kills' making him a Double
Ace. Speaks at World Symposiums
relating to his knowledge of time travel,
quantum physics and the Universe. Is

16 years of age. An Agent and Son of The Entity. Time era origination: Always.

COLETTE ROBERTS-CRAWFORD: The temporal Daughter of Shawn and Christine. Loves to tweak her Father's nose when the latter is mischievous. Has the power to bring individuals back from the dead. An Advanced Fighter Pilot at the age of 10 years old. Precocious, loving and caring for those in need. An Agent and Daughter of The Entity. Time era origination: Always.

JOLIE O'LEARY-CRAWFORD: Cousin to Sir Shawn Crawford through her marriage to Thomas Crawford.

Heir to a billion-dollar inheritance following the sudden death of her Husband Thomas. Time era origination: 2017.

EMILY: A perpetual 12-year old Girl who having ability to conquer Evil by the use of a Medallion with an ancient script. Defeated the Demon along the Narragansett Trail in Gorham, Maine with Sir Shawn Crawford and Tim O'Leary. Overcame another Demon during the late12th Century during the Third Crusades. An Agent of The Entity. Time era origination: Always.

NATHAN DOERFLER: Physician's Assistant who was brought back to life several times by The Entity. Seventh

Degree Black Belt in the Martial Arts.
An Agent of The Entity who has
traveled through time on numerous
occasions to fulfill missions give to him
by The Entity. Holds two Doctoral
Degrees from Georgia Southern
University in Medical Science and
Physics. Cousin to Sir Shawn Crawford.
Stopped the assassination of President
John F. Kennedy in Dallas, Texas in
November 1963. Time era origination:
2017.

ROBERTO "BOB" GONZALES:
Air Commodore for Rotary-Wing
Operations Aviation Helicopter Group,
amicably referred to as 'The Chief'.
Unit Historian and renowned Helicopter
Pilot commanding respect for his

exception helicopter flying skills. Awarded the Distinguished Service Cross and Silver Star for aerial performance of duty beyond all expectations against opposing enemy forces. Principal Paternal Influence and Mentor to the totally irreverent Shawn Crawford. Back-seat Radar Intercept Officer in the F-22B Raptor during anti-drug related missions in South America. Presently serves the Australian Sydney Air Defense Force as the Air Commodore, Pilot of the F-42A Tiger Shark Stealth Fighter, RAH-66 Comanche and AH-1G Cobra Attack Helicopters. Chief Rotary-Wing Instructor for the Australian Sydney Air Defense Force.

ADMIRAL J. HUNTER KING:
Charismatic Special Operations
[SEAL/Delta Force] Leader fluent in
seven languages specializing in Arabic
and Swahili. Seventh Degree Black
Belt in the Art of Silent Killing. Holds a
dual Doctorate Degree from American
University in International Studies and
from the Massachusetts Institute of
Technology (M.I.T.) in Advanced
Fusion Quantum Mechanics. Built his
first mini-jet fighter at the age of 11.
Married to equally charismatic
Kathleen. Veteran of the African Wars.
Time era origination: 2017.

DONALD LAGACE: CIA Operative
and Time Traveler, Agent for The

Entity, Principal Organizer in the operation causing abrupt cessation of the Third World War hostilities in 2018. Part-time Musician and Contributor to famous Scores such as The Star-Spangled Banner. Time era origination: Always.

MARSHAL ALLISON MORRISON: Senior Officer commanding the Australian Sydney Air Defense Base. Wife of Air Chief Marshal Michael O'Leary Outstanding and charismatic Leader of all aerial forces on the Continent of Australia. Directed victory against the incursion of African Federation Forces into Australia. Time era origination: 2074.

AIR CHIEF MARSHAL MICHAEL O'LEARY: Royal Australian Air Force, former Lieutenant Colonel, United States Air Force, Husband to Marshal Allison Marshall. F-42A Tiger Shark Stealth Fighter Pilot and Mentor to Sir Shawn Crawford. Gained Fighter Pilot Ace status when he traveled back in time to conduct aerial battles against aggressors during World War II and the Korean War. Wounded in action. Time era origination: 2053.

SANCHA: The Automated Voice Recognition System aboard the newest Attack Stealth Fighter Aircraft, the F-98A Stingray. Responds only to voice recognition commands given by Sir Shawn Crawford.

THE ENTITY: An Intergalactic Being who is the Champion of Good over Evil. Employs Agents to traverse through a Gateway that enables them to go back into the past and deny assassination attempts on lives of influential individuals who serve only what is Good and Righteous in their own time eras. Utilizes Sir Shawn Crawford as His Agent to correct world injustices. Time era origination: Always.

PROLOGUE

The comet-like mass approached the Earth between the speed of light and sound, circled the planet within 15 minutes and came to rest on the western African Continent. It impacted the Country of Gabon 20 kilometers north of the Capitol of Libreville in the vicinity of Ntoum at approximately 0300 hours. The solid material hit with such force that seismologists around the world registered it as a 9.1 earthquake.

Teletypewriters in capital cities everywhere in the world began 'broadcasting' on the wire that Gabon sustained a tremendous impact from an object from outer space. At first impulse, the estimates before any evidence was proven was that the tiny Country's population of nearly 1,980,000 had to have suffered catastrophically in terms of death toll and infrastructure damage. All in the outside world 30 minutes following the impact firmly believed that no one in the roughly 270 square geographic miles could have survived such a hit with so much force.

 The reality was that the Country of Gabon's population, especially those close to the impact, never felt even a slight jarring of the earth. Telephone calls from outside the Country were ringing constantly in the Parliamentary

Offices in the Capitol of Libreville. The Government Officer on duty attempted to answer each phone call one after the other upon pick-up. There was no answer on the other end each time. The official unplugged every phone in the small building to escape from the incessant ringing. He made a notation in the evening's log relating to what he had just experienced and went into the President's Office, laid down on his cot and went to sleep for the remainder of his watch.

KEPLER 162f

At NASA Headquarters in Washington, DC, the day was just turning into early evening at the time of the mass impact in Africa Gabon. NASA scientists were aware of this episode, but still focused on their primary mission of providing support operations to the International Space Station. Within the Communications Section, dialogue between the Station and Earth receivers suddenly increased no more than 45 minutes following the African seismic event. D.C. scientists had not been oblivious to what occurred on the West Coast of Africa but became immediately concerned due to an unprecedented spike in radio traffic between the Station Commander and Ground Control immediately following the event. The elevated intensity of radio chatter was followed by a sudden loss of all communication. The ability 'to talk' between the Station and earth-bound reception was completely and inexplicably silenced. It wasn't that the communications systems became inoperable for testing showed that the signals emanating between sites appeared to be nominal. Scientists concluded upon examination of the integrity and function of internal circuits that 'talking' back and forth from the Space Station was being interrupted, or intercepted, by an unknown source. They were baffled by this occurrence and could offer no immediate reasoning as to the direct cause of this sudden failure to communicate, or, who and what was the source of this interference.

Trillions of miles away from Earth, a Planet, several times larger than Earth, known as Kepler 162f by Astronomers, was being monitored through the clandestine efforts of an Australian by the name of Donald Canastra. He had improvised his personal astronomy devices to lock onto the Allen Telescopic Array (ATA). This man-made floating 'camera' was the most advanced mechanism used by SETI (The Search for Extra-Terrestrial Integration) personnel in search of discovering life on other planets. What caused him to commit to this unlawful act of using this highly scientific and secret mechanism for his personal use had to do with his dedication to protecting and serving the well-being of all living on Planet Earth.

   Canastra had been a famed Astronomer working for the Sydney Science Foundation to discover extra-terrestrial life for decades. He had Ph.D.'s in Astor-Physics and Celestial Determination. Dr. Canastra had 'fallen out of grace' with the scientific community when he insisted upon, what other local scientists referred to as 'sheer lunacy' in his premonition that the Earth was about to be invaded by extra-terrestrials within the immediate future. It was this incessant insistence of an impending Earth threat that caused him to be 'forced into early retirement' from his government position. His plea for

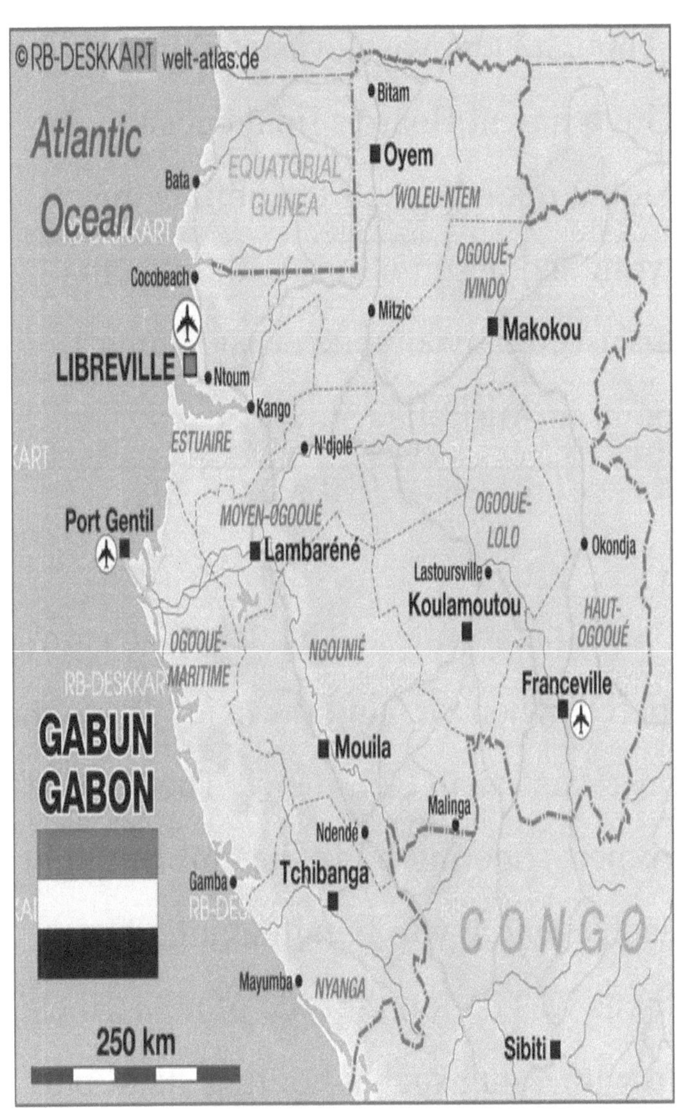

reinstatement was summarily denied.

He was now a 'persona non-grate'.

 Though Don was devastated by the Government Board's final decision, he took it upon himself to continue his work and observations without being discovered by anyone on the highest point in Australia, Mount Kosciusko. Its summit was 7,310 feet (2,228 meters) above sea level and located in New South Wales. This was Canastra's 'perch' when viewing the skies above the vast Australian Continent. The sight of comets shooting by in the ambient light each evening was breathtaking. His focus was not on the side of amusement in witnessing such 'shooting stars' but relegated to monitoring Kepler 162f, the mysterious massive 'look-a-like' Planet light years away.

The Mountain site he had chosen to monitor Kepler 162f was not accommodating. His experience in dealing with frigid conditions, however, was not foreign to him. He had studied the skies on numerous continents, a couple of them less hospitable than the others. Consequently, Canastra's preparations were meticulous. He knew that this sojourn was an indefinite one and so he came prepared with the appropriate shelter. His choice was the MSR Remote 3-Tent Device that offered the following qualities of support for his environmental conditions.

The MSR was a four-season refuge that withstood the harshest of winter conditions. It was designed to handle fierce summit winds and heavy snow loads. The floor plan accommodated three inhabitants, but since he was there alone, the additional compartments were more than suitable for equipment stowage. The MSR's Easton Cyclone poles were nearly indestructible and its Dura Shield-coated fabrics keep the moisture sealed out. In addition, reinforced guyout points provided reliable tension, snow flaps sealed out snow drifts and color-coded pole clips were included for easy setup in any conditions.

Don used a sophisticated device to

create a linkage between his own instruments and those located within the Sydney Scientific Observatory. He had 'borrowed' specific parts from the Observatory just prior to his dismissal. Canastra knew that his predictions were leading to a decision by the Scientific Board to relieve him of his responsibilities. As a matter of protecting the world from what he knew had to be a cataclysmic occurrence being just a matter of time, he surreptitiously took what he needed to further his own examination of the heavens, through the Array's tremendous power thereby allowing him to see well into the cosmos. He alone was able to forecast an event that was to occur. Don Canastra was a genius in establishing new methods to further scientific knowledge, not only in Australia, but also in other world countries.

 Light years away from Earth on a mass of rock named Kepler 162f by the earth-bound scientific community, a beam of light shot outward into Space. This Planet had been discovered within the past 18 months by an organization that searched for celestial entities that supported life for extraterrestrial existence. It was judged to be larger than Earth and rotated around a 'Sun' like our Earth. Its distance from its Star was greater than that on earth and the rotation was twice that of our present world. Twenty-four hours of daylight was followed by an equal time of darkness. From what could be seen and evaluated by the few scientific minds existing around earth, the possibility of life as they knew it was ranked at 85%. Among those top scientists aware of the prospect of extra-terrestrial life was Dr. Donald Canastra.

He sought to enhance his astronomical device so that he could peer as deeply into space and toward the beam as possible. As he focused on his intended area, a second and third beam suddenly appeared in his scope, one after the other. As they were such a distance from earth, they appeared to hang in the sky as though suspended among the millions of celestial bodies in the universe. But Dr. Donald Canastra knew these were not just other stars occurring for their development as beams of light were nearly instantaneous and separate from one another. He pulled away from his scope and murmured to himself, "It has begun."

THE INTERNATIONAL SPACE STATION

The International Space Station serves to detect oncoming anomalies. During the communications 'blackout',

Planet Kepler

momentary confusion reigned aboard

the International Space Station once the

communications system faltered. But that was the only thing that happened for backup systems came on-line to re-establish voice support, especially sides of the huge complex. Perhaps the most notable ISS experiment aboard the Station is the Alpha Magnetic Spectrometer. This device is intended to detect dark matter that is the precursor of something large and menacing advancing toward Planet Earth. It's operation is based upon the complex communications systems that work in concert with one another to establish a "dialogue" further coordinating the ease to which the Space

Mount Kosciusko, Australia

between the Russian and American one

such anomaly would have normally been identified. But since the device was 'down', the very quick 'blip' that would have shown itself through the communications array system did not reveal itself before personnel were able to notice anything unusual at all. This moment of time lost on everyone would prove to be one of the most important occurrences that would be shown to be a failed warning of what was to come to influence earth's very existence.

SYDNEY MARITIME DEFENSE BASE

The ball floated slowly over the netting. Sir Shawn Crawford calculated its trajectory and spiked the ball to the left side of the opponents' side. His Daughter Colette dived for the ball before it hit the soft sand but was too late to control it. It landed out of bounds and bounced off to the side of the court. Colette got up from the sand, brushed herself off and looked back through the netting at her smiling Father. Shawn smiled and wagged a finger in her direction while moving his head in a 'no' gesture. Colette was <u>not</u> pleased.

Shawn's Son Christopher took his place as the next team-member to serve to the ladies on the other side of the net.

Christine, Shawn's Wife, stood next to her Daughter. They looked at one another and slowly nodded. They both knew how their Son/Brother served and thus positioned themselves slightly behind one another and to the right side of the in-play area.

 Christopher hit the ball in the direction of his Mother. Christine met the ball with two hands and lofted it in the direction of Colette. The ball was perfectly placed for a 'spike' return. Colette leaped at least two feet upward and hit the ball squarely and with great force in a downward trajectory directly at her Brother Christopher. He never had a chance as the volley ball came 'crashing down' on him and striking his nose while sending him backward sprawling to the sand below.

 He got up and gingerly tested the condition of his nose. The Boy then looked over at Colette who stood arms akimbo with a devilish smirk on her face. She then raised one finger skyward and shook her head 'no' in the direction of her Father and Brother. Christine burst out laughing as Shawn consoled his Son while examining the nose. Christopher bent down to the sand on his knees and threw up his arms as if in 'surrender'. Shawn then decided that the women in his life possessed a 'threat' to both him and Christopher and called a 'truce' by conceding the game.

A boy approximately 14-15 years of age had been watching the volleyball contest with some interest. He attempted to get Christopher's attention several times during the match, but the latter was too engrossed in the family competition. Finally, Christopher looked over to the sideline and recognized him. He started to walk over to the boy when he was distracted by something his mother had said to her husband,

At that moment, an Air Force military SUV pulled up along side of the court and a young officer jumped out from the front passenger seat. He immediately went over to Shawn and handed him a manila folder that was stamped 'Top

Secret' on the outside. Crawford opened it and read its contents while his Family waited patiently. He then looked at the young officer who had retreated back to the SUV and then to his Family who stood close by.

 Shawn closed the folder and beckoned for his Family to join him in the Air Force SUV. Once inside, the driver gunned the vehicle and turned onto the adjacent macadam in the direction of Base Headquarters. It took less than five minutes for them to arrive. A young enlisted woman wearing a Class A uniform stood waiting. When the SUV screeched to a halt, she opened both the front and rear doors for the Crawford's to exit. Shawn led the way up the short flight of stairs leading to the building and immediately turned to the right.

He and the others behind him were stopped by a Air Policeman who checked their identifications before allowing them up to the second floor. SSG Coffill The Commander's Gatekeeper, welcomed all with a smile as she knocked on the door before opening it for all to enter. Inside the Commander of the Air Base Office were three individuals seated before Marshall Allison Morrison.

Shawn and his Family members took seats around a small conference table located in the left corner of the room.

Each of them was presented a thin folder with the marking "Top Secret" at the center top of the small dossier. They perused the few inside pages and one by one they closed the folders.

 "Who else has seen this report?" Shawn asked.

 The Base Commander, Marshal Allison Morrison, answered by saying that the report was presented immediately from Intelligence and that they were the first to see it. Shawn opened the file again and continued to stare at the content. He then looked over at Christine who had a furrowed brow of both fascination and amazement. Christopher and Colette merely looked intrigued, which was about par for their excitement meter.

 The other members of the group were Air Chief Marshal Michael O'Leary, Morrison's Husband, and Australian Navy Commodore J. Hunter King. Morrison and the other two stared intently at Crawford.

 "What is Gabon's Minister doing about the impact of this object on territorial soil? This happened last evening local time and certainly there have to be some serious questions about the status of the Country and its people."

 Air Chief Marshal O'Leary answered, "This is the conundrum: even though seismic measurement went through the roof everywhere on the planet, no one in Gabon appears to be fazed by such an impact. It's as though nothing happened at all. What we have here on the surface is that a giant-like meteor, or celestial object, impacted approximately 20 kilometers north of Libreville, the Capitol, As far as the Gabonese are concerned, they were left with a monstrous hole, a quarter-mile wide and 45 feet deep. There were no casualties and there is no evidence of any type of radiation.

"The Gabonese Government has not declared an emergency of any sort and, because of the political turmoil presently, is not allowing anyone inside the Country to do any type of scientific investigation. It's the weirdest thing I've ever seen."

 "This isn't the only anomaly we're experiencing. A rogue astronomer, by the name of Canastra, is holed up on Mount Kosciusko with clandestine telescopic equipment that is considered to be some of the most sensitive in the world for studying the celestial sky. He has within the past 48 hours sent a cryptic report that indicated he believed the earth will soon be under attack from alien invasion within the immediate and foreseeable future."

 "Marshall Morrison, how are we involved in all of this?" asked Christopher.

"There is another anomaly that we've yet to share in all of this recent development. In Libreville, this morning, a naked Caucasian male about14 years of age was seen walking along a road leading to the entrance of the home of the Mayor of the City. He was stopped well before he could get to the enclosed compound by the Mayor's security personnel. When questioned by the officer in charge about why he was there and in that immodest condition, the boy merely smiled and pointed a finger toward the Mayor's residence. The security official and the boy looked at one another briefly and the officer then ordered that the boy be allowed to gain access to the grounds leading to the

Mayor's villa. He was then escorted by two Gabonese military personnel into the Mayor's home. By all accounts, he is still there and there has been no word from within the home of the Mayor as to what is happening within the building. The boy identified himself as Kaden."

"Again, Ma'am, how are we involved here in Australia?"

Commodore King then jumped into the conversation. "From what we've learned from the interaction between the boy and the officer-in-charge, the boy appeared to exhibit an intensifying look when focusing on the man. One witness was absolutely certain that the boy's eyes turned color from a bright blue to an intense orange resulting in the individual in charge to be visibly weakened."

 Christopher looked immediately to Colette who returned his gaze with a grim look on her face. Shawn was the only one seated who noted the silent exchange, but said nothing at the moment.

 "What all of that entails is beyond any of us at this point," King continued. "We've been approached by the State Department in Washington, D.C., to see if any of you may have a clue as to what all of this means. Christopher is well-known world-wide for his expertise in quantum mechanics and the workings of the Universe. This implosion of a celestial object in Gabon, the sighting of the young boy in Libreville shortly thereafter, and the actions and warnings noted by Dr. Canastra may all have a thread of connection at this point."

 "Not to mention the communications anomaly aboard the International Space Station," O'Leary added. "They have yet to discern the cause for the loss of radio traffic. Why don't you and Christopher pay a visit to the good Dr. Canastra and see if we can make some sense in all of this going on at the moment."

MOUNT KOSCIUSZKO

Dr. Canastra sat transfixed behind his array telescope. It was after midnight and the wind whipped by relentlessly and he shivered in the cold. He had been in this position for at least 90 minutes searching the sky above in the direction of Kepler 162f. He leaned back for a moment and wondered to himself if he were not already taken by imagination at the thought of extra-terrestrials 'visiting' Earth. Resolutely, he returned to his scope. A moment later, an advanced-looking helicopter flew by the mountain at a lesser altitude. Its search light was on as it canvassed the lower mountain. It briefly went out of sight and then re-appeared, this time closer to his location. It continued to gain altitude and soon flew overhead and out of sight beyond the next crest.

Don knew that the government would find him with their specialized and very sensitive equipment. It was just a matter of time. He thought, however, that his theory of extra-terrestrial invasion of Earth would have been more self-evident, timely in that he could provide proof. Not that any of this mattered.

Suddenly, the helicopter was overhead with its searchlight pin-pointed directed at Canastra. It hovered briefly and then side-stepped to the left and over to a patch of somewhat level ground covered in snow. As it descended to the ground, the snow flew wildly around the fuselage. Once landed, the aircraft wound down as the pilot throttled off the engine. The whine of the turbine slowly subsided and then stopped abruptly as the pilot applied the rotor brake. Canastra noted the missiles attached to pods on either side of the aircraft.

 The pilot-in-command door opened and out stepped, to Canastra's amazement, what appeared to be a young boy of 13 or 14 years of age. The other cockpit door flew ajar and out stepped a tall lean-looking man in an aviator's suit, He had an air of confidence and authority about him, not so much as to display arrogance, but to relay a sense of re-assurance to Canastra that nothing be feared. The boy approached first and stopped some six feet in front of the scientist. The wind whipped his shoulder-length hair as snow flakes began to fall around him. The temperature had to be below 0-degrees Fahrenheit, but the boy showed no discomfort whatsoever. His smile served to disarm Canastra immediately.

 "Hello, Doctor Canastra, My name is Christopher and this is my Father, Air Marshall Sir Steven Crawford of the Sydney Air Defense Force. We would like to talk to you, if you don't mind, about your theory of extra-terrestrial invasion of this planet. As I'm certain that you are fairly feeling the effects of this wind that appears to be picking up, let's step aboard our helicopter and be more comfortable."

Donald Canastra didn't know why he trusted this young man, but he felt at ease all of a sudden. He followed young Christopher to the aircraft's fuselage and jumped into the bay after him. Air Marshall Crawford followed them both inside and sat beside his son. Shawn then offered Dr. Canastra a thermos of coffee that was declined.

Christopher began, "Dr. Canastra, have you heard about the seismic activity reported on the West Coast of Africa lately?"

"Yes, I have. My short-wave radio has

picked up some information about a cataclysmic event that occurred not far from Libreville. Why do you ask and what does this have to do with me?”

 “Because,” Shawn answered, “You probably are aware then that the 'explosion' that hit the area left no trace of damage or destruction to any of the surrounding area. No casualties were reported, nor was there any evidence of collateral impairment of any kind. Don't you think that this was highly unusual?”

 Dr. Canastra looked from one individual to another and then answered by asking a question of his own. “Were there any specimens taken from the site of ground inclusion?”

"I'm not aware of any that were broadcast to have been taken. No, nothing reported as far as we know. Why do you ask?"

"I have a theory that whatever happened in Gabon may be related to what I've been studying light years away from earth. Gentlemen, have you ever heard of a planet named Kepler?"

Shawn looked at Christopher with a quizzical look. His Son merely smiled faintly and looked directly at Dr. Canastra and proceeded to tell him what he knew of Kepler. When he was finished, Canastra looked at Christopher for a long moment. Shawn knew some information had been shared with the

Scientist who had been unaware of much of what Christopher had told him.

Canastra then looked down at the bulkhead floor of the helicopter for a long moment. When he raised his head, his eyes met those of Christopher who merely nodded slightly. All of this was lost on Shawn.

"OK, let's not harbor secrets. Christopher, how do you know so much about Kepler and what is it that I should know about the Planet?"

All of a sudden, a loud whining sound pierced the air and the helicopter rocked back and forth when part of the mountain exploded less than 50 meters from their location. This was followed by two more explosions, and, then, quiet. Shawn and Christopher were already scampering toward the cockpit as Dr. Canastra picked himself up off the aircraft flooring. He started to jump out of the helicopter when Shawn yelled back at him, "Leave the equipment, Doc. We've got to get out of here NOW!"

As the blasts began around them, the aircraft spooled up to minimum rpm and then lifted off sharply to the right and away from the explosions. They were soon out of danger with the helicopter gaining enough altitude to elude any more shrapnel pinging off of the fuselage. Christopher was at the controls and indicated to his Father that all systems were in the 'green'.

Shawn banked the aircraft around 270-degrees and crested an out-cropping of rock and snow and lowered the nose by applying forward cyclic. The aircraft picked up speed and sped down the side of the mountain to a plateau that offered enough room for the aircraft to settle to a hover and land. Shawn kept the engines running at flight idle.

"Alright then, Doc, that was interesting! I know I have a lot of enemies but none who knew enough to know that I was up here on the mountain. Who do you think was targeting us and why?"

Canastra didn't respond right away and

then said, "We all have enemies out there who don't want us telling the truth about controversial issues that compromise the effectiveness of their operation. I have a pretty good guess as to who would not have me share what I know about what is going to happen to our planet in the immediate future. Where are we going and when can I return for my equipment?"

 Christopher then put his hand on his Father's shoulder and said, "Look, 10 o'clock low and one thousand meters. Do you see the moving lights, Father?"

 Shawn looked in that direction and said, "Let's go have a look and see if those moving vehicles might have had something to do with the breaking up of our get together."

 He spooled up the rotors, lifted off, and pointed the aircraft's nose in the direction of the parting vehicles. As he got closer, flashes of light were emitted from the convoy, followed by noticeable sounds of projectiles bouncing off of the titanium fuselage. Shawn banked left. He toggled the gun switch to 'on' and brought the nose to line up with the vehicle that was shooting at them. "Guns", he said.

 A string of tracers arced downward toward his moving target. Aircraft rounds struck the rear of what looked like an armored personnel vehicle. It veered to the right and then violently to the left before being masked by vegetation at the base of the mountain. It re-appeared a second later and Shawn fired a string of 50 mm rounds to the front of the fleeing truck and saw them strike the roof and front causing the driver to lose control. The vehicle side swiped one tree before banging head on into another. The other two vehicles in the convoy disappeared into the tree line.

Shawn banked the aircraft hard to the left and brought it around slowly until it hovered 10 meters above and 20 meters to its front. There was no movement at all around the vehicle.

Christopher then pointed to a spot 20 meters away from the damaged vehicle and Shawn hover taxied over to it. He set it down gently and kept the aircraft at flight idle as he frictioned the controls. They exited the aircraft and approached the vehicle cautiously. Shawn had pulled his 9 mm Beretta from his shoulder holster and led the three to the front of the truck.

There were two bodies lying inert inside the cab. Christopher checked the pulse on each and found one to be still alive, but just barely. In the interim, Canastra followed Shawn around to be the rear and opened up the rear overhanging canvas flap. Inside were unopened three crates each sealed with wire. There were no identifiable markings.

Shawn jumped into the back of the vehicle and tugged at one of the boxes. He was able to move it with very little effort. Undoubtedly, whatever was in these were incredibly light. He decided to pull one of them from the truck and put it on the ground.

In the interim, Canastra went around to where Christopher was administering first aid to a facial wound on the only surviving individual still unconscious inside the front cab. Don watched as the young boy carefully and meticulously applied gauze he had taken from the emergency kit aboard the helicopter to

the man's head. The older man noted
the serious approach provided to the
care of the wound by this young man.
As he watched the hands work, he noted
a soft bluish light being emitted from
the boy's fingertips. In a matter of
seconds, the blood has ceased to seep
through the gauze wrapping and the
injured man started to regain
consciousness. Christopher
immediately sedated him with a peculiar
hold applied to the right side of the
man's head. The boy merely looked up
at Dr. Canastra and offered a brief
smile.

 Shawn came over to the cab and asked
about the injured man. Christopher told
him what he had found and done to

finally keep the individual unconscious. He told his son and Canastra to follow him behind the truck where he had laid out several containers taken from the back of the wrecked vehicle. Shawn had opened one of them in the interim and raised the lid to show the other two present. What Christopher and Canastra saw simply astounded them. They proceeded to carry the containers over to the aircraft and secured each in the rear of the fuselage. They then carried the unconscious vehicle occupant and tied him to a restraint in the rear crew compartment.

 Christopher jumped in the command seat and began the aircraft's start sequence. Shawn sat in the right seat with Dr. Canastra occupying the jump seat to the rear and between them. Don then asked what was the immediate plan and voiced concern about his instruments left unattended on the mountain. With the aircraft slowly lifting off, Shawn told Canastra that they were going back to the site to retrieve what they could from Don's camp, but not until they were assured of their safety.

 "For the time being, we are going back to the Sydney Defense Base. After we have a better picture of what we're up against, then we will decide on a proper course of action. I'm certain our friend back there will be more than happy to tell us what we need to know."

SYDNEY MARITIME DEFENSE BASE

The Leopard taxied into its designated hangar, went into a 2-minute cool-down period and Christopher completed the shutdown sequence by turning off the turbine, battery and remaining switches. Shawn looked back toward Dr. Canastra, nodded and waited for 1LT Caruso, the Leopard's 'Baby-Sitter' to open the main hatch for the occupants to exit.

They were met by Commodore King who stood by a government-issued

SUV. Crawford came over to his friend and introduced Canastra who shook hands with the senior officer. King motioned for all to climb into the SUV to be transported over to Headquarters where the Base Commander and Air Chief Marshal O'Leary were waiting for them in the conference room.

 Canastra was introduced to those present and sat down next to Christopher who shared a brief glance with the Astronomer. This was not lost on both Crawford and King.

 Morrison and O'Leary then entered the conference room as everyone rose to their feet, with the exception of Canastra. After all were seated,

Morrison introduced herself and her Husband O'Leary while pulling a folder from her brief case.

 "Dr. Canastra, I hear that you've been 'enjoying' a bit of an adventure with our notorious 'Ambassadors of the Unknown'", as she gave a side-long glance to both Shawn and Christopher. Crawford merely smiled and kicked his son gently under the table. The two then sported countenances that suggested the highest form of emotional hurt they could muster.

 "We have taken the equipment from the Leopard and are in the process of examining its contents. But, first of all, I want to know what the devil is going on with you living out of a tent in the mountain cold. I have the background of your being dismissed arbitrarily from the scientific community, but I would like to hear from you what has precipitated your little jaunt and excursion to the highest point in Australia."

Again, Canastra shared a look with Christopher who nodded for the scientist to share what information that caused his unusual behavior during the past few days. The Scientist looked from one individual to another before proceeding.

"I'm certain, Commander, that you've been briefed on my removal from all scientific responsibilities due to my absolute belief that the earth's well-being is in jeopardy via an impending invasion from species arriving from the Planet Kepler. Indeed, Keplerians have already arrived here and are preparing for the main wave arrival of their military forces in the very near future. I know. I get the look of disbelief on your faces, with the exception of Christopher. What I'm about to tell you can be corroborated by this young man sitting next to me. After all, and no offense to Air Marshal Crawford here, Christopher and I have been communicating with one another over the previous three months about this very issue."

  Shawn looked over to Christopher with

a furrowed brow and a look of incredulity. His son merely returned the gaze with the hint of a smile. *I'm certain there is more to follow with my Father following this meeting*, he mused.

Let me begin with saying that I have been in contact with a Keplerian here on Earth for several months now. Christopher is familiar with this being who calls himself Joshua. Marshal Crawford, whether you remember or not, you met this young man during the failed attempt by Sir Robert Lindsey to overthrow the British Government several years ago. Joshua was part of an advanced party of Keplerians whose responsibility was to gather strategic intelligence prior to the Keplerian main-body arrival.

 "Joshua should not be taken as a nemesis, but rather a tool for informational flow concerning the real reason the Keplerians are advancing toward Earth. There is a maleficent faction on Kepler that fancies itself as plutocratic innovators in furthering and strengthening the Keplerian existence. They have become increasingly powerful as a force, having made inroads into the planetarium government through sedition and brute strength. Their main goal is to invade and subdue Earth's powers-that-be and establish a base of operations here on this planet. Their end-game, once they have accomplished their mission is to create a weapon that will alter the very existence of our solar system.

 "Kepler's sun is burning out. The Keplerian existence is in jeopardy. As they have been to Earth countless times in the past, as evidenced by their support given to ancient civilizations in the building of the pyramids, for one example, they were perceived as a benevolent people. Their footprint is significantly noted around the globe. They established a base of operations that molded into the society that is the fabled *Atlantis*.   From there, they sent emissaries to every corner of the globe and continued to further their well-being and good will toward Earth's people for over a thousands years. They were welcomed everywhere on this planet.

"When their scientific community established immutable evidence that their planet was doomed with the death of its sun in time, they began to search for an alternative domicile for their inhabitants. Naturally, Earth was the ideal location as its atmosphere and living conditions mirrored their own on Kepler.

"Then, a certain group known as 'Affitatum' formed and led by one who was called Krixus. This was a man who once led their battle forces against invading elements from their own solar system. His positive status with the

Keplerian Government and their military ceased when he was found to manipulate the scientific community into working for him with the ultimate goal of subverting the Government. His lust for ultimate power was so encompassing that he felt invincible. Had it not been for the young man Joshua, Krixus would have then succeeded in his plan to become Kepler's first Dictator. He was discovered attempting to sabotage their power grid and placed in their prison system for life. Or, so, it was supposed to be.

 "Krixus, with the help of loyalists, managed to escape and went into the planet's mountainous terrain where he began to gather enough sympathizers to mount a successful attack on the Keplerian hierarchy. Once he gained absolute power, he showed no mercy to the pre-existing body of governmental officials and had them all executed. His wrath was boundless.

 "Does any of what you are telling us relate at all to the event in Gabon, West Africa?" asked King.

 "It has everything to do with the impending invasion by Krixus and his armada of ships heading toward Earth. There was nothing plausible or even possible with the lack of destruction that the object left behind. It defies all scientific knowledge that such an impact could leave no trace of damage to humanity or infrastructure other than a deep crater. As we speak, scientists from around the world are preparing to examine this anomaly with little regard for protocol. Knowing that an object of such size impacting the earth with such velocity would surely raise some crucial questions regarding the blast effects, would it not?"

There was momentary silence in the room. Christopher then spoke in a tone that caught everyone's attention. His demeanor was stoic, but resolute in the way he responded to Canastra's prior revelation of this potential cosmic invasion. As he spoke, he turned toward his father and rendered what was easily the most serious countenance ever shown to his paternal figure.

"I have known of what Dr. Canastra has related for some time. All of what this Scientist has said is true and soon to come to fruition. Joshua and I have had meetings in the past several weeks unknown to all of you. He has been in our midst for nearly two years. Since the London attempt to take over the government by extremists, he and I have been in contact with one another. He has kept me up-to-date with the circumstances surrounding the hierarchy take-over on Kepler. Until recently, there has been no concern for the well-being of Earth and its inhabitants. But, even now, there are advanced Keplerian elements at work here on our Planet in preparation for their armada's arrival. Krixus is well armed, prepared and clandestinely equipped with agents in place to mitigate any immediate earthly response to his invasion.

 "Father," he said to Shawn, "Joshua was at our volleyball match when we were summoned to Headquarters the other day. I started to go over to him when I got distracted by the sudden appearance of the military sedan arriving to take us to meet with Commander Morrison. We had planned to meet the following day so that I could be briefed on Keplerian developments. The recent turn of events obviously put that on hold."

For a brief moment, no one spoke. Then, Shawn turned fully in his chair and looked his son in the eye. He stared into the boy's eyes for a long moment before speaking.

"Why have you not mentioned this to me when you initially were knowledgeable of the potential events facing us?"

"My FATHER told me to keep all information to myself. HE said that all would be revealed at such a time of HIS choosing. HE has been working behind the scenes in an attempt to pr-emp the attack through HIS own channels. There is much you do not know about our Protector, The Entity. HE understands that information presented prematurely would lead to catastrophic consequences for all on Earth. There are forces at work, Father, that are well coordinated to initiate such a global confrontation too unbelievable to grasp. I trust HIM, as I know you do as well, Father, that we will be guided to do the right thing at the appointed time."

 At that moment, there was a knock on the conference room door. Sergeant Coffill apologized for the intrusion and said that Dr. Canastra's equipment was now secured and on its way back to Sydney. Don thanked the young lady and turned toward the others around the table.

"Now that I have been somewhat vindicated through Christopher's informational background regarding an impending invasion of Earth, I would like to continue my investigation into the heavens. I feel that I can be of use in terms of the arrival sequence of the Keplerians.

"For now, however, I am completely exhausted and would request suitable quarters where I may re-group my strength, grab a shower and get something to eat."

That's when the lights flickered and went out.

INVASION FLEET

Krixus' armada was steady on course to intercept the southern parallel that crossed the continent of Australia. His plan was to bring the Australian authorities to its knees through a show of brute force. He possessed over 200 spaceships with all transporting over 500 rebel soldiers. Once established over the Earth, the ships would break to a specific location in the world thereby covering every major leadership venue. There, the spacecraft commanders would make their demands for either surrender or suffer the wrath of the might of the Rebel armada's awesome firepower.

 Krixus knew that to destroy the infrastructure would be a major tactical error. He would use all weapons at his disposal if necessary and he realized that taking over the Government without firing a shot would mean so much more of an advantage for his people than having to destroy what he would have to re-build for his own use.

 His title was 'Emperor' and he lived up to it body and soul. History would show that leaders of his ilk ruled with the thought of inspiring fear so that those under him wouldn't question his actions to achieve his goals. And Krixus was indeed ruthless.

During the Keplerian takeover, Krixus assassinated over one thousand key political adversaries. His actions 'persuaded' those left leaderless to pursue a course of action that coincided with continuing to draw breath rather than to stand up and be eliminated. With all of the warlike behavior, Krixus was a shrewd tactician and understood that negotiation, his negotiation, could sometimes be the panacea for survival for the affected invaded locations.

Australia would be the test bed for predicting success. If he encountered minimal opposition from the reigning government, the likelihood of a successful outcome would be insured. Each of his other spaceships would not proceed to force a surrender from their assigned Earth governments without the express consent of their Emperor. Krixus was adamant about this order. The leadership under him was loyal and would obey every demand made by him to afford a comprehensive takeover of the planet. He knew his Planet Kepler was dying through the erosion of its sun's energy. The Keplerian Planetarium Council knew that it was a matter of time before all life would be extinguishcd with the loss of their sun. They debated without resolution time and time again in terms of a solution for their continued existence. Nothing was ever resolved,

 One of the Council members had

suggested to approach Earth's leadership to request wholesale migratory assistance from Kepler. The idea began to take root because of Earth's similar living conditions to their own Planet. Krixus had been a member of that Council and knew that negotiations with Earth's government officials would end in a standoff. This loss of time to save Keplerian life would be the precursor to population extinction once the sun's energy gave out. He decided to take matters into his own hands. He planted the seed of sedition through rebellion by insisting that the government's decision-making process was inept and that he could provide a tangible solution, but needed the assistance of those who believed in him to support his plan without reservation.

LIBREVILLE, GABON

Earlier that day, the Mayor of Gabon sat transfixed by the presence of the boy, Kaden, clothed, in his office. Three security guards with weapons stood attentively around the room. The Gabonese Chief Military Officer stood to the Mayor's left with the Minister of Defense to his right. Mayor Omar Dimbano eyed the boy suspiciously and with curiosity. Kaden stood before the Mayor's desk and displayed no emotion while staring directly into the eyes of Dimbano.

 "Who are you, boy, and why are you here?" the Mayor began.

 The boy remained silent. Then, he raised one finger and pointed it at the General to Dimbano's left. A laser-like arrow of energy shot out like a dart and pierced the heart of the Chief Military Officer who fell dead back against the wall.

 The Mayor immediately got to his feet. His three guards threw their safeties off of their weapons, aimed and each fired a round at the boy. The projectiles fell harmlessly to the floor by Kaden as though he were protected by some invisible shield. The young man then turned to each guard and quickly and methodically pointed his finger at each man. Again, a laser of energy was emitted at his fingertip and hit each individual squarely in the chest. They all crumpled dead to the floor with eyes staring blankly open. Kaden turned toward the Mayor and stood before him silently as if waiting for something.

 The Mayor and Minister both had backed up with arms raised as if to implore the boy to stop his actions. After several moments, the boy turned around and calmly walked out of the office.

 He proceeded out of the building and

began walking along the thoroughfare leading to the edge of the city. He was not followed.

 Mayor Dimbano and the Defense Minister were paralyzed with the fear of knowing that their lives had been spared for no apparent reason. They both looked around the room at what was left of the four bodies hideously contorted in their painful deaths. Neither moved for what appeared to be a very long moment. Dimbano was the first to take action as he picked up the telephone, screeched into it and slammed it back into the cradle. He then turned to the Minister and saw that the latter had passed out four feet in front of the Mayor's desk.

Outer office guards poured into the room and stood aghast at the sight of the bodies lying everywhere. An officer immediately went to the Mayor to insure that he had not been harmed.

 "Mr. Mayor, what has happened? Who did this?"

 Chief Executive Officer of Libreville turned his far-away gaze to the officer and merely said, "The Devil."

SYDNEY MARITIME DEFENSE BASE

The lights flickered back on after a few

moments followed by the sound of sirens heard by all in the room. Shawn got up from the conference table and ran to the door. He was the first outside and stopped quickly. What he saw completely amazed him. In the far distance by the shoreline, fires were raging at the Maritime wharf complex. Huge billowing clouds of smoke rose into the air. Then, the first explosion was heard followed by another. Several more occurred as the quay was consumed by thick black columns of smoke. More emergency vehicles were heard in the distance as they meandered their way to the wharf area. Shawn stood there in complete disbelief.

 He turned around and saw the others

standing together in a tight group. Morrison was on her cell phone and most likely talking to the Emergency Reaction Center located in the heart of Base Operations a few blocks away. She looked at Shawn and motioned for him to come over to her and the group.

 As Shawn turned to join the others, he detected a glint of sunshine that appeared to bounce off a metallic object in the sky above. He stopped in his tracks and peered intently in the direction of what appeared to be a shiny object, stationary in the sky and approximately 5,000 feet above the Base. In an instant, the anomaly shot to the right and then rose vertically with tremendous speed. It was out of sight in mere moments.

 He turned and joined the others as he continued to scan the skies above for any reappearance of the object. When he reached the group,

 Morrison told him that a catastrophic chain reaction-like series of detonations had occurred for no apparent reason. The wharf area was completely destroyed and there were multiple casualties found lying around nearly everywhere. Morrison told him to get airborne in one of the Base's advanced stealth aircraft and execute a complete reconnaissance of the Base and the Sydney surrounding area. He was to report back to her immediately upon his return.

 Crawford raced to a nearby vehicle, jumped in and started to drive off as the passenger side door opened and his Son Christopher jumped inside. Shawn hesitated for a brief moment, smiled faintly and floored the accelerator. The military sedan sped off toward the hangar 2 minutes drive away. They both got out of the car and ran into the bay where the aircraft was waiting. 1LT Will Caruso, Shawn's Plane Captain, was there to facilitate the startup procedures and to insure that the futuristic looking aircraft got airborne safely. Christopher jumped into the pilot seat to the right as Shawn strapped on his harness in the command pilot's

The Leopard Advanced Tactical Military Stealth Aircraft

adjacent left seat. He quickly spooled up the three jet engines and immediately began a taxi sequence with the Tower personnel. Receiving instructions from the Tower about wind direction and speed, he maneuvered the aircraft to the nearest active runway. Shawn looked over at his Son who merely nodded. Crawford pushed forward on the throttles and the Leopard appeared to leap into the sky after a very short distance down the runway. It quickly leveled off at 5,000 feet above ground level (AGL) and began a circular route around the greater Sydney area below. They were in the air for no more than five minutes, when both Shawn and

Christopher heard a very familiar voice come over their intercom system. They looked at one another and smiled. This was going to be the start of an adventure never experienced before in their lives.

ABOARD THE LEOPARD STEALTH AIRCRAFT

In the cockpit of the Leopard, Shawn had responded to the voice he heard come over the intercom. It wasn't one of the controllers in Sydney, but an old familiar tone that caused both Shawn and Christopher to prepare for an adventure that would change their lives in a most unimaginable way.

The voice was that of The Entity, an intergalactic Being who championed good vs. evil. HE employed Agents within the Universe to traverse through a gateway that enabled them to go back and forward in time to correct wrongdoings, such as assassinations, and turn the course of history for the betterment of society in the future. He utilized Shawn as HIS Agent to correct past, present, and unforeseen future injustices. The Entity wasn't from a specific planet or location, but was from everywhere.

"Your Blueness," said Shawn looking over at Christopher. "To what do we owe this distinct pleasure? It's been quite a while since we've heard from you. We were wondering the other day if you had retired to a Tahiti hut somewhere out there in the cosmos. How are the wife and kids?”

 “Shawn, you always had a way of making me chuckle,” the voice responded. And, hello, Christopher, my Son! Has this 'renegade' been good to you? I know that Lady Christine has well taken care of you and Colette since I've been away. You've grown, my Boy! And, Shawn, you are your still immutable self, full of bravado that was founded on the righteousness of the human spirit.”

"Your Vastness, please, I do believe I am blushing," replied Shawn. Christopher giggled as he looked over at his father who responded by raising an eyebrow in his son's direction.

"Shawn and Christopher, I have an immediate assignment for you both that is of great personal interest, not only to myself, but to the other Beings existing on another planet. You both may have heard of it by name, Kepler."

Christopher slowly nodded in recognition of the name. Shawn merely looked at his Son and was not surprised that the latter seemed to know all about the Earth-like Planet. This thought would, of course, develop into another conversation with the boy at another time.

 "Just what do you have in mind for us, Your Hugeness?" Shawn asked.

 After what seemed like an endless giggle, the voice continued in a more serious tone. "Your Planet Earth is about to receive some most interesting visitors from Kepler. There is one individual currently studying and watching movements by Keplerians who have launched an armada of ships that are heading toward Earth. They are not coming for a visit, but to make themselves home on your Planet. Kepler is a doomed Planet, my young friends. A cataclysmic event will occur soon. You both have a mission of great importance. I leave you now with the faith in knowing that all will be right in this world as you prepare to engage the visitors from Kepler."

 And with that, as he always did, The Entity's voice ceased and his presence was no longer felt inside the cockpit. Instead, the aircraft immersed itself into a bluish-looking cloud. The fuselage shook for what seemed like an eternity, but was affected by the mist by no more than 15 seconds. The advanced jet aircraft exited the cloud into clear airspace and over territory that was foreign to them both. This was no longer Australia. Nor did they feel they had transitioned into a spatial environment that anyone, for that matter, could identify.

Shawn looked over at his son who had a knowing smile. Shawn merely took the look in stride and sighed. Nothing ventured, nothing gained.

THE QUESTILLIAN BOUNDARY

They brought the Leopard out of altitude to get a better look at the terrain below. It was a frozen wasteland. As far as the eye could see, the ground level was crusted with several feet of ice with large chunks of rock sticking out of the land mass like Popsicle sticks. They were jutting upward in a random pattern. But at a closer inspection, there seemed to be a pattern to their placement. And they were symmetrical in an odd sort of way.

 From their nine oçlock position a futuristic fighter crossed 25 meters in front of them at an incredible speed. It banked hard to the right to maneuver behind the Leopard. Shawn knew an aggressor when he saw one and this guy wasn't in the area to invite them to dinner later on. As a matter of fact, it looked all too well that the aviator wanted to have THEM for dinner!

 Shawn brought the nose of his fighter

vertical and climbed quickly to 10,000 feet AGL. The "bandit"followed closely behind and fired a missile that canted to the left of the Leopard's fuselage at the last second.   Shawn reacted by dumping the nose and turned the aircraft to the right in a steep dive. He continued his turn and pulled up 10 meters above the frozen ground. Christopher was looking to the rear to find the aircraft.

 "Father, he's off our 8:00 o'clock position and trying to turn into us," Christopher shouted out.

 Shawn brought the Leopard back to the left with G forces that ordinary pilots couldn't withstand. Christopher kept his eyes on the intruder and pointed him to Shawn.

 "There he is, Father! Moving within our line of sight now at 11:00 o'clock."

 Crawford shifted the nose of the Leopard slightly to the left and told Christopher, "Fox One!" The missile left the aircraft in a blur and homed in on the rear of the aggressor's fuselage. There was a blinding explosion as pieces of aircraft disintegrated in front of them. Shawn banked hard left to escape the debris and kept it coming until he had completed a full circle. He flew over the wreckage and saw no sign of life.

 What was that all about, thought

Shawn. And the aircraft. Never seen one so advanced looking since the Leopard. Who was that guy? And why did he try to take us down? Questions with no answers, for the moment.

As they descended even lower to 100 meters above ground level (AGL) they turned the nose of the aircraft 90-degrees to the left. As they pulled out of the turn, in the far distance, a kilometer or less, there was an out-cropping of ice that appeared rectangular and no higher than 3 meters above the landscape.

Shawn brought the Leopard to within 50 meters with the object on the advanced aircraft's nose. He climbed to 250 feet AGL and flew the aircraft in a circular pattern around what looked like a building in the middle of nowhere, wherever this 'nowhere' was. On top of the roofing that was glazed over with ice crystals were identical sticks, or antennae, situated on each corner of the building's structure. As Shawn brought the aircraft to fly directly over the rectangular object, the Leopard suddenly lost power.

Christopher immediately lowered the landing gear in time for the Leopard to settle on the iced-laden floor. Shawn engaged full flaps while Christopher thrust the powerful engines into reverse. When the aircraft came to a stop, Shawn looked over at Christopher as if to say what in the world just happened?

His Son unbuckled quickly and retreated behind the cockpit to exit the aircraft. Shawn followed and before they opened the door, Shawn abruptly grabbed Christopher's arm and told him to listen. The Leopard was being peppered with objects from an outside source. The sounds got louder and louder.

Shawn told Christopher to get back into the pilots' station and begin aircraft start sequence. Crawford had no idea if the Leopard would even respond after the catastrophic engine failure.

Just then, a familiar voice came over their intercom and told Shawn to stop the start procedure. The Leopard shuttered into life and immediately came to full power. Without Shawn or Christopher at the controls, the jet aircraft began moving forward and picked up speed rapidly. It was soon into the crystal clear cold atmosphere and climbing to altitude. "You have the controls, Shawn," the voice finally said through their ear phones.

 As the jet aircraft gained altitude, Shawn went over in his mind what had happened on the frozen tundra below. He became irritated as frustration grew at what he couldn't comprehend. He peered through the Plexiglas in front of him as Christopher continued the climb to 5,000 feet. He felt as though he was running away from something that he shouldn't ignore. If it hadn't been for The Entity, there is no telling as to the possibility that they would still be on the surface below, and, in what condition.

He grabbed the controls and made a positive transfer with his Son Christopher. The latter looked at him with some amusement as he knew exactly what his father was thinking. Shawn Crawford was a warrior, a man of action whose life had been dedicated to completing the mission, the assignment. Christopher knew exactly what Shawn was intending to do and therefore prepared the aircraft for landing.

GABON, WEST AFRICA

The Mayor immediately sent out the military to capture Kaden and bring him into custody, if that were even possible, he thought to himself. He told the Defense Minister, who had collapsed in total fear, to get up off the floor and find out who this boy was and why he was here. The Minister, with ashen face, nodded quickly and left the Mayor's office. An hour later, the Commander of the Mayor's Military Guard, came back to the Mayor's office and said that there was no sign of the boy anywhere. He had simply disappeared.

Meanwhile, Kaden, cloaked invisible,

stood at the edge of the city limit along a dusty roadway and watched intently in the direction of the Gabonese Capital. He had watched several military vehicles scream by him, but unable to be detected. The rear of the vehicles held six Gabonese military personnel with AK-74 assault rifles, three on each side of the rear bed of the vehicle. They were looking intently to their front for any sign of the boy. Ten minutes later, they came back toward him and rushed into the city. Kaden merely smiled, however faintly. These beings are completely helpless, he said to himself. Then, in a moment's instance, he left his location by teleporting over to the crater where the 'object from space' had hit the earth.

He went down one of the sides into the lowest point of the impacted earth. He must have been 40 – 50 feet from the surface level when he reached into the blackened soil and took a handful of the dirt and rubbed his hands together vigorously. He continued to do this for at least 90 seconds and then abruptly stopped. Kaden dropped the contents of his hands to the floor of the crater and stepped back a few feet.

A few brief moments passed. Suddenly, the small mass of soil congealed and began to grow in size. It continued to form into the guise of a humanoid specter until it reached a height of approximately 74 inches. It had two arms and legs with a slim body and well-rounded head. Its eyes were jet black and blinked several times before coming to rest on the boy. It immediately knelt before the smaller figure as in recognition and remained motionless.

Kaden reached over and touched the strange form on the forehead. It reacted quickly by shape-shifting into a snarling beast the size of a gigantic wolf. It was massive in size and stood ready to lunge at the boy. He held up one hand and the animal lay down before him with an almost pleading look in its eyes not to be harmed.

Kaden left the beast and walked over to another area of the crater's floor and molded another humanoid into shape. This one, he left as looking like a normal earthling about 6 feet tall, slender build, blond hair, blue eyes and a kindly countenance. The boy then turned to the wolf and motioned for it to advance to the human's side. As the beast pulled along side, it sat obediently down and looked forlornly up at the form beside him. Kaden then telepathically told the earthly being and wolf-like animal to leave. They immediately turned and climbed up and out of the crater and were gone from sight in a matter of moments in the direction of the Capital, Libreville.

Little did the citizens of their capital city know what was in store for them with the arrival of their new found 'guests'. The invasion of the earth had just begun with the first of the Keplerians making themselves at home, whether they were welcomed or not.

 Before Kaden disappeared into thin air, he reached down and grabbed two handfuls of the scorched earth. Instead of putting both hands together, he ground the soil in each fist and let the residue fall back onto the floor of the crater. He stood back and smiled. This virus would soon be a pandemic and consume humanity in very little time.

Experts and technicians from around the world began flying into Libreville four days following the meteoric impact 20 kilometers from the capitol city. The airport was filled with make shift transports, two and a half ton vehicles and Land Rovers. The commercial aircraft had been arriving, emptying its occupants and materiel and lumbered over to wherever it could find an open spot on the airfield's apron. Scientists from all over the world arrived to study this anomaly that had obliterated the physical crust of the earth, but had left no impact upon indigenous personnel or its infra-structure.

One group that had arrived earlier than most of the teams transported some futuristic-looking equipment, small in nature, and light enough for one man to lift and place in the bed of a pickup truck. A middle-aged man stood by watching the vehicles being prepped for departure. Another came over to him and asked him a couple of questions that were answered quickly and succinctly. The second man turned abruptly and walked briskly over to the vehicle, climbed into the passenger cab side and buckled himself in. When the truck began to move, the crates in the rear started to rattle in the back as the truck moved over the uneven roadbed. It soon reached a comfortable speed once upon the macadam and proceeded in the direction of the crater. The two occupants would soon regret ever arriving in this unforgiving part of West Africa.

THE QUESTILLIAN DISCOVERY

The Leopard came to a stop two kilometers from the rectangular object just visible in the distance. Shawn and Christopher donned heavy white clothing, thermal-insulated gloves and tinted ski masks. The surface was crusty and easy to walk on without difficulty.

"Father, where did you get this

clothing?" Christopher asked.

" I knew our Ethereal Friend would
insure that we were protected from the
elements. There was a container in the
aft section of the Leopard that I
somehow knew we wouldn't be left out
in the cold."

Christopher smirked at his Father's pun.
Shawn Crawford was never lost for
words even in dire or unknown
circumstances and situations. This was
a trait that endeared him to so many.

They approached the roof of the
building that at sea level, if that was
were they were topographically, was
nearly ten feet in height. There was no
sound other than the wind that

periodically howled. With Shawn in the lead, they started to circle the structure. Christopher noted the lack of windows while looking for an entry point. He reached out and touched the surface of the building's side. It felt warm to the touch. The surface wasn't smooth, but rather pocked in a methodical manner. As he rested his gloved hand on the wall, he felt a vibration and almost sensed a hum emanating from the inside.

 He passed his father and stopped some 8 feet in front of him. Christopher reached out to the wall and pressed an area in the middle of a pocked triangle with his forefinger. The 'wall' moved inward some three feet and then moved to the left and out of sight. There was nothing but darkness in front of them at first. As their eyes acclimated to the loss of light, they felt a warm rush of air hit their faces.

 "Christopher, do you have a flashlight with you?"

 His son reached into his pocket and produced a small pen like flash. He gave it to his father and said with a smile, "The Entity is always prepared, isn't HE, Father?"

 "Yes, HE is, Christopher. I wouldn't have minded so much if HE had at least let us in on what happened when we first landed. Can't dwell on that now. Let's try to make some sense of what's in this structure."

 He shown the light ahead and saw emptiness at the end of what looked like a long corridor. He took off one of his gloves and touched the surface of the first side wall they came to, some 3 meters to their front. It was quite warm to the touch, but not overwhelmingly so. He also felt a vibration that seemed to penetrate his hand when in contact with the surface; Shawn withdrew his hand and began to walk along the darkened corridor.

 As he put the light onto the wall to his left, he noticed some strange lettering that were placed horizontally along the top bordering the ceiling. Crawford stopped and ran the flashlight along one of the rows of markings and found some were repeated periodically. A language of some sort, undoubtedly, he mused. He began to move forward and went some 5 meters when he sensed that Christopher had not followed behind him.

"Christopher, what is it? Talk to me."

"Father, I know these figures on the wall. They are indeed a language and one that I do believe I am familiar with knowing. Please don't ask me how I can read what the markings show, but for some strange reason, I am able to decipher what is being said.

Christopher began to read out loud.

"Cherish the human spirit; protect against injustice; recognize the goodness in others; remain steadfast in beliefs; sacrifice for the homeland."

"Doesn't seem to be too radical an approach toward commitment to organizational and personal values. There's more writing on this opposite wall. Can you make out what it says, Christopher?"

"Leave no Keplerian behind; fight for personal freedom; isolate personal fear for the commitment to the goals of Keplerian survival."

"Interesting beat change. On one hand, there is selfless behavior and goodwill and, on the other hand, there is a warlike thread toward anyone who would do harm to the collective group. Christopher, what do you know about Planet Kepler and the Keplerians?"

 "Father, I am drawn to the notion that Kepler is a sister Planet and that it was once a neighbor to Earth. When I say, "neighbor", I mean literally next door type. Earth and Kepler were twin planets existing within a short shuttle ride from one another. Keplerians and Earthlings shared their knowledge with one another for the betterment of both societies. Scientific knowledge of the universe was known to both civilizations. Each had a moon and the same sun to sustain life. They even looked like us. In terms of making a comparison as to which culture was more advanced, there was no question that Earth lacked the achievement that Kepler attained through their diligent pursuit of commitment to overall goals. To admit that Earth lagged behind was not a bad thing. The difference in intellectual growth was choice-oriented. Earthlings focused largely on commerce as opposed to the Keplerian pursuit of scientific dominance. Please don't ask me how all of this has come to me. It appears to be latent knowledge."

While they were talking quietly, they came to a hallway that turned off in a 90-degree angle to the left. They stopped and waited a few seconds before turning the corner. As Shawn stepped ahead, he immediately stopped and took a step backward. They had company. Two distinct voices were heard as if the individuals were carrying on a conversation. Shawn could not make out what they were saying because he couldn't understand the language they were using. He turned to Christopher and whispered for him to get in front of him and try to pick up on the gist of the discussion.

 The speech was not guttural, but similar in tone to what was used on Earth. Christopher listened for a few moments and then the discussion ceased. The two beings retreated behind a panel in the side wall.

"Father, they were talking about our arrival in the Leopard when we first arrived. One of them admitted that they could have been wrong to pepper our aircraft without knowing what our intentions were in coming to this place. They appear to be envoys sent by their higher command to monitor the arrival of the invasion force. One of them described Krixus, the invasion's Commander, as a ruthless killer who stops at nothing to achieve his end goals."

"Hands against the wall, both of you," a voice barked behind them. The demand was in Earth's English language leaving no doubt about what was required of them. Three individuals, a man and two women, appeared out of the darkened corridor with no intent on having them for noon tea.

 One of the women grabbed Shawn's extended arms still on the wall and brought them down behind his back. The second woman did the same to Christopher. Both Shawn and his Son reacted quickly by turning and sweeping their legs toward those of the women. The female soldiers went down to the floor heavily. The male soldier took a step backward as if anticipating a kick from one of the two and leveled an ultra modern weapon at both Shawn and Christopher.

Knowing when to quit while still alive,

Shawn told his Son to put his hands against the wall as initially instructed. The two women had recovered by this time and tied both men's hands behind their backs with corded restraints. They were then pushed down the corridor where they had first noticed two men conversing. A side panel slid open and Shawn and Christopher were ushered into a large room that was bathed in red light. There were cubicles on either side of the room. In the center was a table with odd-looking tools spread out on its surface. In one corner was what appeared to be a sophisticated radar scope. The flooring was uneven and pocked marked

 The side wall slid open and a young

man about Christopher's age came into the room attended by two well-armed soldiers. As the light was a soft red, Christopher didn't recognize the youth at first. But then, he knew the other immediately.

 "Joshua," he exclaimed. "What in the world are you doing here and please tell me that we are not being held captive."

 Joshua came over with a smile and told one of the women to take the restraints off both Christopher and his father. When his arms were free, Christopher went over to Joshua and gave him a huge hug. They stared at one another for a brief moment before Joshua turned to Crawford and said, "It's good to see you again, Sir Shawn. Please accept my apology for the way you were treated out in the corridor. My people take security very seriously and we weren't quite certain if you were here to do us harm or not. By the way, Sir Shawn, that was a bit of fantastic maneuvering to shoot down that rebel jet. Those pilots are known to be excellent air-to-air fighters. We've sent a team out to identify the unit designation that put that aircraft in the sky."

 He then turned to the others in the room and said, "People, here are two of the most outstanding Warriors on Earth's planet. May I introduce to you Sir Shawn Crawford and his Son Christopher. The latter is progeny to

The Entity and lived once among us a very long time ago on Kepler. Although I feel certain that this comes as a surprise to Sir Shawn in terms of his Son's original birthplace. Christopher's father is a renown martial arts expert with a seventh degree black belt in Wing Chun. I can see that his expertise was not lost on our two female soldiers over there in the corner.

 "Please, both of you join me in my quarters for a cup of tea or something stronger." He then turned to one of his soldiers and ordered him to see to the Leopard aircraft outside. A storm was coming and Joshua wanted to insure that the jet was "buttoned up" prior to the weather deteriorating.

Joshua asked his "guests" to make themselves comfortable once they entered the quarters. The room was spartan-like with a small table in the middle and 4 chairs around it. There was a cot in the corner of the room with bedding neatly folded on top of a pillow. Joshua brought over a couple of mugs and a decanter filled with tea. He poured some of the fluid into two of the mugs and handed them over to Shawn and Christopher.

He turned to Christopher and said, "You might remember the flavor of this tea. We both had a cup when in London last. I seem to recollect that you thought that this was the best tasting tea ever."

Christopher took a sip and smiled. "Yes this is the one. Where did you come by this way up here, wherever we are?"

Joshua chuckled and said, "You and Sir Shawn are on the Planet Kepler. Your Father, The Entity, transported you here through the dimensional gateway so that we might meet and talk about how we can 'dissuade' Krixus from invading your planet. This place is an outpost primarily hidden from those loyal to Krixus. When you landed, we thought you were part of those who had taken over the Keplerian Government. Hence, the peppering of the Leopard. I know that I will be having a 'prayer meeting" with The Entity. He saved you both by taking over your aircraft.

 "Krixus' forces will be arriving on Earth within the month. There is a movement in place located in Gabon, Africa to initiate a catastrophic biological attack on your planet. The object that struck was not a harmless meteorite, although it appeared and reacted as one. One of Krixus' emissaries was sent to Earth via this 'device', for it was indeed a capsule designed to self-destruct 5 minutes after impact. The Keplerian left the craft just before it detonated. He made his presence felt when he confronted the Mayor of Libreville by assassinating several high ranking officials in the Mayor's office. The boy, naked at the time, simply left the building and disappeared after walking out of town.

 "The explosions at the Maritime Base that got you both into the air and eventually here through the gateway were caused by Keplerian advanced guard. The purpose was to measure The Base's response to an emergency situation.

 "In addition, when communications aboard the Space Station were knocked out, the culprit was an advanced ray of light that penetrated the known communications spectrum on Earth. That light was generated by the lead ship of Krixus' advancing armada. It served to confirm that Earth's communications could be compromised with the scientific tools possessed by Keplerians.

"I invite you both to spend the night here. The storm has hit us and there is no way you are able to access The Entity's cloud to return to your present-day Australia in that mess out there. Let's meet again in 6 hours to talk about what options are available to stop the invasion from happening. Drisel, one of our soldiers, will take you to your room."

They put down their tea and walked into the spacious room where they first met. Drisel, dressed in battle gear, asked them to follow her. When Shawn and Christopher were alone, they looked at one another for a moment before Shawn spoke.

 "All of this is not a coincidence. It's obvious that The Entity brought us here to map out a strategy to stop Krixus from attaining his objective. At this point, I'm not so sure that I have a clue as to what course of action should be taken. What about you, Christopher? Do you have any insight into this problem?"

 The boy simply smiled and said that all would be made clear very soon.

CRATER SITE, GABON WEST AFRICA

The commercial vehicle pulled up to the crater's edge, stopped and its occupants exited. The two men donned special suits with a breathing apparatus attached. They went to the rear of the truck and took with them a couple of small scientific instruments. They strapped these to their backs and started down the crater. One of the men slipped and fell head long into the soft dirt, rolled over a couple of times and finally stopped his fall. The other man went over and helped him to his feet before continuing down the side of the crater. Much of the soil had penetrated his mask.

When they reached the floor some 45 feet below the surface, they unpacked their scientific instruments and proceeded to the center of the crater. While one of the men planted a vertical pole-like apparatus into the soft soil, the other began collecting samples from the crater itself. They continued with expected and assigned duties for the next 15 minutes when one of the men, the one who had fallen down the slope, began to scream. He then began to take off his protective suit. When his breathing apparatus was removed, the other man looked at his screaming partner with horror. The face of the scientist began to deteriorate. His face turned an ashen color and then appeared

to melt away into a rush of white sand.
The man, or the suit, simply collapsed to
the ground. His partner pulled the suit
toward him and felt nothing of the man
inside. It was though he had melted
away into crater soil.

He immediately turned to leave the
crater when a young man with an animal
stood facing him not 3 feet away. The
youth had blond hair and was well over
6 feet tall. The dog beside him was
massive.

As the scientist began to speak and ask
for help, the dog pounced on the
individual with such force that the
victim fell quickly onto his back into the
crater's soil. His mask went askew with

the force of the dog's blow. The youth
called for the dog to heel which the
animal did quickly. The scientist
struggled to get up, but was unable to
move. He soon started screaming as his
face too began to disintegrate. Within a
few seconds, the screaming stopped and
what was left on the crater's floor was
an empty suit. The youth then turned
and climbed out of the crater with the
animal on his heel. The suits of the
scientists then burst into flames until no
evidence of their prior presence existed.

THE QUESTILLIAN OUTPOST

Shawn rested fitfully on the small cot in the room. Christopher appeared to be in a deep sleep. Crawford swung his legs out and stood on the pocked marked floor. It was dark within the room and he felt a vibration through his feet. He started to go to the door when he heard a voice call out to him.

"Shawn, it's your favorite Entity." Then there was a hearty chuckle.

"Your Hugeness, what a pleasant surprise. I thought you had taken a very quick vacation when we didn't hear from you after you got us into the air yesterday. Or, I think it was yesterday. What would you have us do for you, your Bloatedness?"

This was followed by a hearty laugh that appeared to move the room from side to side. "What will you come up with next, my good Friend?" Another chuckle followed. And then, "Christopher, you're awake!"

The boy grinned in the dark knowing all too well that this banter would continue for a few more minutes. Finally, The Entity said to Shawn. "I have a mission for you both. I know full well what is going on with Krixus and his armada. You will be instrumental in stopping this madman from ever reaching Earth. He will never succeed in dominating Earth. I am sending you to the leader of Kepler's resistance where you will initiate a plan of counter-attack that will essentially defeat Krixus and his minions. I leave you both now as Joshua approaches your room with word about how you will achieve your mission. Know that I will always be with you both." The Entity was then gone and the door opened. Joshua entered the room.

SOLARIUM EXPRESS

The XPT train left the Melbourne Station en-route to Sydney right on schedule. The train is the fastest in Australia operating at a speed well over 100 mph. It connected two cars filled with the lethal compound solarium, a solid mixture that interacted with the air to create a decomposition factor that acted quickly on the surface of living tissue. The container cars were placed to the rear of the train unknown to railroad supervision. The workers who made this happen were Keplerian advanced guard who had been in the railroad system for two years. They were trusted employees who had displayed exemplary work in the performance of their duties over the time of their employment. This action of mobilizing the compound for its rail trip to Sydney was their only task. The men, 7 in all, were free to leave Melbourne and join the other Keplerian advanced party personnel at a rally point at an unknown location somewhere in the world. This meeting point was to be given out within the next 48 hours as a set of coordinates to be provided in the following morning's national newspaper in the form of a cipher. Once all had arrived at such rally point, their duties were to prepare and support the invasion effort through subversion of electrical and mechanical grid throughout the area. All in all, there were over 500 personnel who had been entrenched in world society and who were well trained to carry out their mission before them.

Sydney was not the only area targeted for human annihilation. Major cities throughout the world were also listed for

incursion by the rogue Keplerians.
Similar means to overcome each
populated area were in play to
systematically eliminate command and
control and communications systems
everywhere. Beijing, Washington, D.C.,
Berlin, Paris, the Kremlin and other key
targets were in line to be
organizationally sabotaged and
compromised. Once total control of the
Earth had been achieved, a new Order
was to be established with Krixus as the
head of the organizational hierarchy.

QUESTILLIAN RESISTANCE

Joshua led Shawn and Christopher out of the building after passing through several corridors. A modern looking land vehicle was running next to the doorway. They all jumped into it and they proceeded across the frozen landscape for a little less than an hour's drive. At the outset, Shawn asked Joshua where they were going. He informed them that they were driving to the Keplerian resistance headquarters. Joshua had spoken to the Entity last evening and was given specific instructions to ferry his guests to meet with resistance leaders to discuss courses of action to deter Krixus and his invasion forces from ever reaching Earth.

A half hour into their trip, they were fired upon by a low flying futuristic aircraft. Rounds exploded all around them as the vehicle swerved left and right. After making its initial pass, the aircraft started to come around and make another attempt to destroy Joshua's vehicle.

Joshua told everyone to get out immediately and to run to an outcropping to the right front about 15 meters away and slightly uphill. As they secured positions that offered very little cover and certainly no concealment, Joshua and his driver took out their hand weapons, prepped them to fire and waited. The aircraft made a run on the vehicle. As it lined up to fire its cannons, Joshua's driver fired his weapon first at the on-coming aircraft. A laser-like bolt of energy thrust forth from his gun and hit the aircraft's fuselage in the center and just below its right wing-let. The craft exploded and fell to the frozen tundra 25 meters from their vehicle. There was no sign of movement from what was left of the pilot's cockpit.

Joshua and his driver got as close to the burning wreckage as possible and noted the aircraft markings. The driver jotted them down on a piece of paper and the two of them motioned for Christopher and Shawn to join them at their vehicle. They climbed in and continued their journey toward the resistance encampment.

 The vehicle came to a stop next to what looked like 3 small Quonset huts. They exited the vehicle and walked up to the central hut. No one had said anything on their remaining ride to their present location. Christopher had merely looked at Joshua who returned a meaningful look. Shawn looked at both of them and wondered how much they knew of what was going on with the aerial attack and whatever else the rogue Keplerians had in stock for them. The answers would come at their own time and place. Hopefully, this would be sooner rather than later. Although Shawn did his best clandestine work and operations in the dark, he was strongly opposed to having his mind struggle with any and all unknowns. It was time for clarity and a sense of purpose.

They entered the hut and found several Keplerians working a myriad of scopes, charts and transparent data boards upon which they shifted and manipulated information with the movement of their hands. Shawn was impressed with their studious approach to their tasks at hand. As a matter of fact, no one gave them the slightest look when they entered the small building.

Joshua went over to one of the men who was talking with a woman in the center of the room. The latter individual looked over and saw Joshua approach and smiled. The boy reached over and gave the woman a big hug in greeting and said, "Hello, Mother. This is Sir Shawn Crawford and his Son Christopher. They are here to learn about the invasion process and what to expect upon its initial impact on Earth, if it indeed gets that far. Sir Shawn, Christopher, this is my Mother Lady Lynn, the Leader of the Free Resistance movement against Krixus and his forces."

 Shawn immediately noted the grace with which she moved her extended hand. Lynn was, Shawn guessed in her late 30's, dark blond hair worn short and a model-like face and figure to match. She wore a flight suit and bore the wings of a master aviator on her chest pocket. Shawn was struck by her beauty. Christopher shook her hand and noted his Father's speechless moment and said to Joshua's Mother that they were pleased to meet her.

"I am honored to meet you both. Sir Shawn, you have my utmost admiration for the way you protect against injustice and demand the very best in people, all with a humorous take on life. Yes, I know of you both for the Entity has kept us largely aware of your exploits completed on HIS behalf over the years. When the time is appropriate and this rebellion mess has been taken care of, I would like to sit down with you and your lovely Wife Christine and catch up on the great work you have been doing for the Entity over the years," she said.

 Shawn Crawford was at a loss for words for a moment, blushed and told her that it would be his honor. "Lady Lynn, thank you for that. I wouldn't have accomplished so much without the presence of my Son Christopher to help guide me along the way."

 "We all know Christopher, Sir Shawn. Being a Son of the Entity, Christopher lived among us up until he was 3 years of age. The Entity's mandate that we share him with you and Christine was not a surprise, but a tribute paid to you and your Wife for all the good that you do in your world. Please come with me into the adjoining room and share some food with us."

Joshua excused himself and approached a military individual making notes on the transparent data board. He filled in the officer with what had transpired during their trip regarding the attack by the rebel fighter. He passed along the notes taken by his driver so that the officer could record what rebel aviation unit was responsible for the incident.

After Shawn and the others were seated around an oval table, Lynn asked a mess steward to bring in the food from their kitchen located to the rear of the building. The fare was modest and filling. While they were eating, Lynn asked Shawn about what he knew of Krixus and the purpose the latter had for the invasion of Earth. He responded by telling her of the meeting in Sydney in the Commander's office with Dr. Canastra and that the scientist had filled them in on the impending invasion, his knowledge of Krixus gained from information provided by her Son Joshua and his premonition that the Keplerian uprising here on her Planet was a precursor to overtaking and defeating Earth's political and military process and prowess. That the Keplerian sun was burning out was a chief reason for Krixus' actions despite all efforts to reason with him to approach Earth leadership with their inevitable dilemma of extinction. Not to be diminished in the mix was Krixus' ego and his strive for power.

Then, the military officer Joshua had shared information with came over and whispered something into Lynn's ear. She nodded once, got up from the table and excused herself to go into another room. The officer followed her and closed the door behind them. Christopher looked at Joshua for a long second and then said, "There was something specific about those aircraft markings wasn't there, Cousin?"

"One of the elite rebel aviation units is located 25 kilometers due east of here. Our location has seemed innocuous to their overflights as these buildings had been deserted for years. We've been careful not to leave vehicles in the open in the event one of the aircraft does a recon in this area. We have a 'spotter' on the hill overlooking their airbase who radios any takeoffs and their direction of flight. He or she changes locations for observation purposes along that ridge line every 4-6 hours depending upon the aerial activity below. We generally have a 10-minute window to 'clean up' our base of operations by concealing vehicles and equipment before any aircraft arrive. They have thermal imaging to detect any heat signatures in the area they are assigned to scout. Our buildings have a lead compound in the walls that negates their opportunity to discover any of our personnel or materiel. Thus far, we have been fortunate not to have been discovered because of the conscientious work done by our forward soldiers and those here on the ground.

"The aircraft we encountered today represent their best of the best. Our mission is to monitor movement of aircraft and personnel from that airbase and feed such information to our satellite bases located throughout a 100-kilometer radius. We represent only one cell of hundreds all over the planet whose mission is to gather intelligence regarding their movement, strength and suspected purpose as they try to eliminate us one cell at a time. My mother is very good at making sure that our base of operations remains undetected."

 "Who is in command of all of these cells and what are they doing with the intelligence they gather from groups such as yourself?" asked Shawn.

 "We submit what we know through a clandestine communication system that is manned by specialists. The intelligence is forwarded from there to a higher command, whose location and leader is unknown to us. From what we've learned, the data is collected from all of the cells and a course of action is taken against the rebel forces. The 'big' picture is viewed at this highest level where operational control of our forces is maintained. We hear bits and pieces of successful raids on rebel locations as a result of data fed up the chain of command. What we do seems minimal, but putting together all aspects of intelligence gathering, we are able to make a difference in the fight to overcome the rebel hierarchy."

"What kind of aviation assets do you have at your disposal to combat the air threat" asked Christopher.

Joshua then told the two to follow him. They exited the building and walked some 10 meters to the rear to a fence that was secured with a lock. After going through the barrier, Joshua took the two to what looked like a huge mound of crystallized ice, perfectly formed. After clearing off some of the snow on the right hand side of a wall, Joshua unlatched a key pad and punched in four numbers. The door swung inward and they entered the 'building'.

 Inside was a massive hangar with several aircraft sitting silently on their pads. Maintenance personnel were all over the futuristic fuselages performing their daily inspection of each 'bird'. The aircraft was part rocket and part fighter with two huge turbines to the rear. Joshua took them over to one of the aircraft and put one foot on the ladder leading up into the cockpit.

"This is the Razor. It's our interstellar fighter that is relatively new to the inventory. Its maneuverability is unparalleled even giving your Leopard a good run for its money. There is enough room for three inside the cockpit. Let's go inside and have a look, shall we?"

Joshua led followed by Shawn and Christopher. Once inside, Shawn saw that there were three stations, one for the pilot, co-pilot, and flight engineer. He looked at the instrument panel and quickly deciphered the logic behind the placement of avionics, systems and controls. He was almost salivating looking at the interior. Christopher saw his Father's look and merely smiled.

This was a 'candy store' experience for someone like Shawn Crawford. Joshua nudged closer to Shawn and handed him a set of keys.

 "Sir Shawn, why don't you and Christopher take the Razor for a spin. She hasn't flown in nearly two weeks and has already been prepped for flight. You look comfortable with seeing the layout of key switches for you have a bit of a drool on the side of your mouth."

 Christopher burst out laughing! He knew his Father was in 'aircraft heaven' for Crawford welcomed any challenge of flying something he had never controlled in the air before. Shawn looked over at Joshua for a long moment and said, "You're serious?"

"Dead" replied Joshua. "I had called ahead last evening and asked that the aircraft be available for a 'test' flight this afternoon. Can't think of anyone else who might want to see if this aircraft performs according to specifications other than yourself. Are you 'up' for it?"

Shawn looked down at the systems instruments and control panel. He quickly understood that the fighter was not a runway-oriented craft but gained its altitude initially through rear thrusts putting the fighter in a 'helicopter hovering mode' before actually launching.

"I will certainly give it the old college

try. Do you have renter's insurance?
No, just kidding. I promise to take care
of any dents and dings incurred during
the test flight. Christopher, what do you
say? Interested in a new experience
with dear old Dad?"

RAZOR FLIGHT

 Joshua gave instructions to his
maintenance team below as he climbed
down out of the cockpit. Within
seconds, the roof of the hangar began to
slide open revealing a crystal clear blue
sky above. This was lost on Shawn as
he was strapping himself in and looking

over the way the switches were laid out. He knew that a certain sequence for engine start was universal for all aircraft and quickly began flipping toggle switches. Shawn looked outside the cockpit and was surprised to see that all had left the hangar as the engines roared to life. He lowered a lever and the engine nacelles rotated downward. All of a sudden, the aircraft rose slowly into the air toward the opening in the roof. He applied more thrust and the Razor literally jumped into the air and was at 500 feet above the ground before Shawn leveled off. The aircraft hovered at that altitude for 15 seconds before Christopher reached over and lifted the lever and the nacelles rotated to a horizontal position. As Crawford had already applied thrust, the Razor leap forward with tremendous speed. Shawn looked over at Christopher who merely smiled and said, "Sorry, Father, just trying to help?"

 Crawford was in his element. He brought the nose of fighter vertical and added thrust. The jet shot up quickly to 20,000 feet and leveled off. He pulled back on the power and the fighter cruised with hardly a sound noticeable. Christopher could tell that his Father was beyond thrilled.

 A jet fighter flashed across their windscreen from right to left followed by another. They banked to the left and attempted to come around behind the Razor. Shawn switched his armament to missiles then banked left in a steep turn to keep the rebels from lining up on him to the rear.

 Then, Shawn turned to the right and dumped the nose of the fighter. He and Christopher fought the G-forces upon their bodies to the extent that they almost passed out before Crawford brought the Razor out of the dive.

 Christopher immediately scanned the skies to locate the fighters. Shawn tapped him on the shoulder and pointed a finger in the direction of their 12 o'clock. There, low on the horizon, the first of two aircraft was just making a recovery and attempting to level out. Crawford didn't wait for another opportunity. He fired a missile at the lead fighter and saw the ordnance explode mid-section. The rebel aircraft broke into two large pieces and plummeted to the frozen ground below. The last aircraft attempted to fly out of the 'kill' zone, but was too slow to react. A second missile came off the rail and struck the remaining fighter just aft of the cockpit. There was nothing left of that fighter as the wreckage dropped heavily to the ice below.

 Shawn looked at his Son and declared the test flight over. He banked the Razor to the right and took a heading that put them on final approach to the resistance location 10 minutes later.

SYDNEY MARITIME DEFENSE
BASE AND BEYOND

Shawn's delay in returning to the Defense Base was not unusual. King guessed that he received a mission from The Entity en-route and that he would be gone for awhile. He and Crawford went way back to the early days when they were both assigned to the same unit in Maine on a Temporary Duty Status (TDY). They hit it off immediately and found common ground like coaching Little League. They did so for two years and thus referred to one another as 'Coach' when in private.

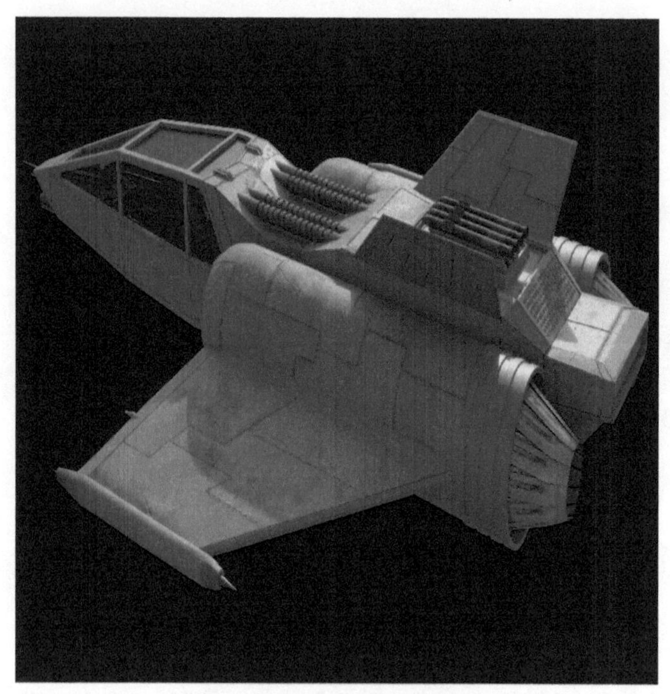

The Razor Fighter

Shawn had trained Hunter King as a helicopter pilot. The latter did so well and picked up flying so quickly that he routinely took the Commander's helicopter on a training flight, as well as out to the range to fire missiles and Gatling gun ammunition. He was meticulous in his training and soon developed a reputation as one of the leading experts in gunnery warfare.

On this day, he 'coerced' Air Commodore for Helicopter Operations, Roberto "Bob" Gonzales to go flying with him to the northwest of Sydney. They were into the flight for about 25 minutes when they heard a familiar voice come over their intercom. It wasn't an aircraft controller.

The Entity introduced himself to them both with a hearty laugh that caused them to look at one another as to wonder what did they do to deserve this visit. No matter what the reason, there was always an agenda with The Entity that required attention.

"Bob and Coach, what a wonderful surprise to see both of you flying together. It's been too long since I've had a chance to talk to you both. I have a mission for you that requires your attention in assisting our Friends Shawn and Christopher.

Coach, you were correct in surmising that I have sent them on a mission of great importance. They will explain to

Rebel Fighter Aircraft

you what is going on as it relates to Krixus' armada movement toward Earth. As always, your actions reflect great worth toward protecting what is righteous and good in this world."

And, with that, HE was gone and the aircraft entered a bluish-looking mist. The helicopter shuddered for nearly 10 seconds before coming out in clear air and over frozen tundra terrain. Off to their left front was a series of small buildings in the middle of nowhere. A sleek looking fighter, more a spacecraft, was making a final hovering approach to the rear of the buildings. It settled nicely onto the white crusted ground as the engines spooled down. Bob brought his aircraft in to the rear of the other craft and landed some 10 meters away. They were immediately surrounded by ground troops carrying futuristic rifles. They weren't in Kansas any more.

 A soldier came forward and signaled for them to exit the aircraft. They did so as several firearms were focused on them. At that moment, Christopher was the first to leave the spacecraft and recognized the Cheyenne Helicopter as Sydney's property. He ran over as Hunter was getting out of the aircraft first and gave him a huge hug. Everyone immediately put their weapons down when Christopher exclaimed, "Uncle Hunter, what on Kepler are you and the Air Commodore doing here! It is so good to see you both!"

 By then, Shawn had climbed out of his aircraft and jogged over to where his friends and Christopher were talking and immediately wrapped both of his arms around Hunter and Bob. "You gentlemen must be lost! I know that I've taught you navigation well, Hunter, but how in the world did you wind up here on Kepler? No, don't tell me. A mutual Friend 'requested' your services while you out boring holes in the sky back in the Sydney area. Please come inside and fill me in on what's been going on back in the 'other' world."

 Joshua walked with Shawn and the others on the way to the building and said, "We heard a lot radio chatter on the net about an aerial battle. What do you know about this?"

 "Yes, I'm afraid our little test flight turned into a 'fur ball' of a get-together with a couple of rebel fighters. We managed to shoot down the two that jumped us. There were no survivors."

 "Sounds like we can expect more and more aerial traffic coming this way, now that several fighters have been 'downed' in this general area. Get with your friends, Sir Shawn, while I brief my mother on what happened during your flight."

 "Roger that. I can fill you and the Commander in whenever you want.

Really not much to tell. Talk to you later." He left Joshua and walked over to Bob and Hunter who were busy talking with Christopher.

LIBREVILLE, GABON, WEST AFRICA

The supervisor of the two men who had gone to the crater attempted several times to reach them on the radio with no luck. Since this was unusual and protocol dictated prompt communications between all company personnel, he sent a vehicle with two more personnel to the site. When the man and woman arrived, they got out of their vehicle and walked over to the truck parked by the crater's opening. After searching in and around the vehicle, they walked over to the crater's edge and peered down to the bottom. They saw the scientific instruments that the previous two had taken with them, but there was no sight of the two men who initially traveled to the crater. The woman did notice two areas of scorched soil at the bottom of the crater. In the mix looked like the remnants of headgear bottom, however. This was the last thing that they noted before a huge beast set upon them from behind, knocking them both down into the crater below. Very soon afterward, two more bodies burst into flames on the crater's floor. They had neglected to radio in their findings when they first arrived.

INTERNATIONAL SPACE STATION

Lieutenant Commander Brock Holt's shift had just begun when he was told of an anomaly portrayed on the station's far-reaching telescopic array. Holt went over to the Finnish technician at that station and asked what was going on. He was told that they had picked up movement of multiple objects far out into space. The analysis of this anomaly showed that the mass of objects was heading toward Earth and that, if left unchecked, would arrive at Earth's doorstep within 10 days.

"Who else is aware of this, meaning has this been reported to our ground station on the planet?"

"No sir," replied the technician. "Even though we've noted the mass of objects approaching for the past 48 hours, we thought that it represented the space clutter that we see all of the time up here. But this group of whatever it is appears to be too well coordinated and uniform to be a random set of debris. I thought I would let you know immediately."

"OK, thanks. I'll let Control in Houston know what we've found. Stay on it and let me know if you feel that this may turn out to be a threat of any kind."

RESISTANCE HEADQUARTERS

Shawn told his 'uninvited guests' to join him in his debriefing outlining his encounter with the Rebel Fighters. Both Bob and Hunter were shivering the cold weather. At the same moment, Christopher had gone over to the Cheyenne and was returning with heavy parkas for each to wear. Hunter looked at Christopher and asked where those had come from on such short notice.

"Uncle Hunter, you must know that to underestimate the ability of The Entity to provide in all matters of circumstance

is to deny the day of your birth. HE always insures that whatever materiel is needed to conduct and complete a mission will always be available. Father and I were the recipients of such clothing when we were unapologetic ally transported here to this Planet. We just go with the flow, Uncle Hunter," Christopher said with a smile.

They were almost to the entrance to the building when Hunter said, '*This Planet*' did you say, Christopher?   What does that mean exactly?"

"Coach," Shawn interjected, "Looks like you're going to miss out on Beef Wellington Night at the Officers' Club in Sydney tonight. You, my Friend, are walking on frozen tundra located on the Planet Kepler. I know it's hard to believe, but you and Bobbo here are interplanetary travelers courtesy of our mutual Acquaintance, The Entity. Ask me if gets any better than that."

 "Does this really mean that there is no Beef Wellington tonight for dinner?" asked Hunter with a wry grin.

 "No, my hungry Friend, but I hear the soup and bread of the day are to die for here!"

 When they entered the small

conference room where the Commander
Lynn and her cadre were waiting,
Shawn made the introductions to all. He
embellished, but truthfully, the exploits
of both Hunter and Bob from past
missions. Hunter merely rolled his eyes
and Bob gave him an evil look.
Christopher merely chuckled. Hunter,
Shawn and Bob were like Brothers and
would do anything to preserve the very
bond that served and protected them
over the many years. As Shawn had
mentored Hunter, a former US Navy
SEAL, so too did Bob Gonzales instruct
Shawn in the ways of flight and
battlefield survival. As a matter of fact,
their first encounter together with The
Entity was over South American terrain

during a drug cartel mission. They were
transported back in time to the day when
General George Custer met his demise
at the Little Big Horn. When they
returned to their accurate time, they
found it difficult to explain to the
Aviation Maintenance Officer why there
were two arrows sticking out of the
fuselage! It only got better from there.

 Joshua called everyone to be seated or
stand if they so desired. He asked
Shawn and Christopher to fill them in
on their encounter with the two Rebel
fighters during the routine 'test' flight.
Shawn told them that they were jumped
very quickly by the two bandits
followed by their fighter pilot instinct to
counteract the threat. Christopher added

that the second fighter attempted to flee the area after its wing man was shot down. There was no radio traffic that they were aware of between their pilots and their flight following. At least nothing was broadcast over their channels.

 "They've lost several aircraft over the past 48 hours. It doesn't take much to figure out that their aerial competition has become severe. Our spotter at the airfield has noted increased support aircraft activity. They are going looking for their downed pilots so we can expect to see more over flights in this area," remarked Lynn.

 "Mother, I think it's time we became

proactive and take the fight to them," said Joshua.

 Several of her officers agreed with Joshua. They were tired of playing hide and seek with the enemy. Their airfield installation was easily mapped out so hitting their communications and logistics areas using guerrilla-type tactics initially followed by an aerial bombing of their tactical operations center would certainly neutralize this site.

 Lynn turned to her senior commander and told him to draw up a plan of attack in two stages at the airfield within the next 24 hours. She wanted an operations order prepared within the

Rebel Invasion Fleet

next 4 hours that outlined the present situation, mission and execution, logistics and command and control.

The tactics used were at her discretion as directed by higher authority. There would be no discussion with the leadership above her station regarding her intent to dismantle the enemy's flight operations. This one was on her and her alone.

The meeting broke up and Shawn approached Lynn immediately thereafter. He told her that he and his now team of three others would offer any assistance she felt necessary to achieve her goal of neutralizing the enemy in the air. She acknowledged his gesture and told him to find the chief of maintenance operations in the hangar for further instructions. Shawn thanked her and went over to the other three who were talking in earnest with Joshua.

 "Were cleared to assist this operation by providing aerial support. Bob, how much ordnance did you bring with you through the gateway."

 "I have a full load out. Hunter can sit in the gunner's seat and provide air to ground Gatling gun support of the ground operation and I have tactical missiles on board that will neutralize larger targets.:

 "That's great, and we can use the Cheyenne's firepower. I was thinking of using the Leopard in the fight as well. Christopher, I am sending you back to where we left the aircraft and have you fly it over to our location. I know I've been cleared to fly the Razor and together with the Cheyenne and Leopard, we ought to create a large enough dent in aircraft and runway operations to neutralize any opportunity for an aerial counterattack on the part of the rebels. Any questions?"

 "Coach, I feel I may be better utilized by assisting the ground unit through sabotage methods. My SEAL training will come in handy with munitions placement and overall stealth. Bob can do everything necessary in the Cheyenne, so he really doesn't need me," replied Hunter.

 "Sounds like a plan, Coach, but promise me you'll keep your head down. I still owe you a dinner at the Officers' Club when we return and I don't relish the idea of having to eat alone," Shawn countered.

 Christopher and a driver departed for the outpost in a little less than an hour. The day was bright and cold. They were into their trip about a half-hour, when a convoy of three vehicles approached them from the left. The markings on their trucks identified them to be rebel forces, probably on patrol. Christopher's SUV-like vehicle showed no markings, thereby identifying them as resistance owned. The driver started to out run them, but the rebels were much too fast. Christopher and the driver were intercepted in a matter of moments. "This is not going to end well," remarked the driver.

 A junior officer exited his truck and walked over to where Christopher and the driver sat in their vehicle's front cab. He walked around their SUV and stopped in front of the driver's side. The officer motioned for the occupants to get out and told them to put their hands on the vehicle. Another rebel soldier came over and kicked the driver's leg from behind. The latter went down to the frozen ground in tremendous pain.

Christopher reacted quickly to this treatment by swiftly bending down and, at the same time, swinging a leg toward the soldier's heel. The rebel went down hard on his back and hit the back of his head on the icy surface causing him to be momentarily dazed.

The officer started to pull out his weapon when Christopher thrust his right hand outward toward the individual. A pulse of blue light hit the rebel in the chest and he went down to the ground unconscious. Four rebels attempted to fire their weapons at Christopher at once, but the latter shielded himself and driver when a crystallized bubble surrounded them. The rounds fired were repelled by the clear protective mask and simply dropped to the ground.

 Christopher then extended his arm toward the four soldiers and the rebels froze in place as a blue light consumed all of them.   Seconds later, all four soldiers dropped heavily to the icy terrain.

 Christopher helped the injured driver to their SUV and put him in the front passenger seat. The boy then got behind the wheel, started the vehicle and raced off in the direction of the resistance outpost. The driver looked over at Christopher in disbelief at the latter's actions and said, "Who are you?"

 The boy just smiled and continued to

drive without saying a word. They soon came upon the Leopard that had been shielded from the previous storm with a thin composite material. Christopher got out of the vehicle and over to the fighter where he began taking off the covers. Once this was done, he instructed the driver to get what was necessary out of the SUV and to climb into the Leopard's cockpit's right seat. Once they were ready to initiate a start sequence, Christopher told the driver to sit back and relax. The Leopard was soon up to full operating power and took off seconds later. It took them only five minutes to reach the resistance headquarters.

  After landing, Christopher shut the

engines down and he and the driver exited the aircraft. Shawn and Hunter were waiting for them at the front of the fuselage. The boy helped the driver over to the building to check on the status of his leg as the other two followed and asked questions along the way.

 "What happened, Christopher?" Shawn said.

 "Father, we were intercepted along the route by three rebel vehicles. Before they could fully detain us, I neutralized all six soldiers. The driver had been kicked pretty hard and before they could do us further harm, I did what was needed to protect us both. Rebel headquarters will be sending out others to find out what happened to their patrol when it doesn't check in when they're supposed to."

 "OK, nothing more we can do about that now. Go check in with Joshua and get something to eat. Following that, gets some rest. We're pulling out of here on the ground at midnight. Our mission at the rebel airfield takes place at 0100 hours. Here is a copy of the Operations Order. You have the Leopard. Review the Opord thoroughly and, if you have any questions, don't hesitate to ask. I'm glad that you're alright, Christopher. Your mother would have me drawn and quartered if you got hurt out here!"

THE SOLARIUM TRAIN

The Express came into Sydney on time. Passengers got off the train carrying their luggage and proceeded into the terminal. Keplerian rebels were there waiting for it and detached the final two cars from their couplings. Another engine approached them from a side track and slowly backed into one of them. One of the rebels hooked up the cars with the engine and the three cars began to move away from the station. They came to rest some 100 meters and out of sight of the main station.

The rebel leader instructed the others where to place the detonators. They worked quickly and soon had all of the explosives in place. They trotted over to an adjacent maintenance building and secured Hazmat suits, put them on and waited.

While they were in the building, a railroad guard patrolling the area with his German Shepherd noticed the two cars and engine sitting idly on the side track. That area wasn't supposed to be used for traffic at all because the rails were old and splitting through years of use. The guard got on his radio and called in the presence of the isolated train with main dispatch. The supervisor on the other end of that call told the guard to go over and investigate. Meanwhile, they were going to send over an engineer to get those cars off of the dilapidated track and into an area where they could be inspected.

 The German Shepherd started to whine and bark while focusing on the train. The guard tried to calm the animal down with no luck. Finally, the dog lunged ahead as the man lost his grip on the leash. It ran to the second car and started jumping up and down wildly, The guard called a second time into Control and told them what was going on. The Shepherd was trained to sense the presence of contraband on trains. When the guard came over to the dog, he immediately saw the detonators attached to the cars. He called in a third time and the supervisor told him to get away from the area immediately. Ten minutes later, an elite bomb squad arrived wearing appropriate clothing and began going over the cars thoroughly. When they found each detonator, they examined it carefully and within a matter of moments were able to neutralize all of them. By this time, the yard was swarming with local police who began a search of the yard to include its buildings.

The rebels had seen what was going on. They took off their suits and quickly left the area. Hazmat gear was left on the floor. The rebel leader and the others were met by an innocuous van that came to a screeching halt and picked up all of the men. One of the officers noticed the van rushing away from the area and told his supervisor. The latter got on the radio and connected with a police chopper that had just arrived on the scene. The pilot acknowledged the call and saw the vehicle heading toward the highway. He alerted other units in the area relating to the location and direction the vehicle was heading. Ten minutes later, the van ran into a road block just prior to getting on the highway and subsequently detained. The personnel were taken to the police station and separated into different cells so that they could not communicate with one another. Australia's equivalent of the FBI and Central Intelligence Agency were called in to question those detained. Their FBI represented the 'good' cops in this scenario and the CIA personnel the 'bad' cops.

 The leader of the group was not ascertained up front, but with a little CIA persuasion, using their own methods of interrogation, the leader's name soon surfaced. That individual was immediately taken into a room with a single chair to which he was tied. A woman CIA agent came in and questioned the man about what the operation was all about and why were they there in the first place. At first, he wouldn't say anything, but with a little persuasion, some fingernails pulled with needle nose pliers, he tended 'to soften up'. After 15 minutes of excruciating pain, the rebel finally gave up and told the woman about the entire operation involving the dissemination of solarium into the Sydney atmosphere. Other rebels began 'to offer' what they knew and before long, the puzzle was completed.

 CIA personnel reported their findings to Sydney's main office who in turn telephone Washington, DC to inform them of the global threat. Phone calls were then made to the major world leadership hubs. A global search then began to identify railway cars traveling with passenger units in major cities everywhere. Many of those found were harmless; over 75 of them had cars that were loaded with the deadly compound solarium. Washington DC coordinated the overall effort of communicating the threat to every major city in the world. Finding the Sydney train totally saved the world.

GABON, WEST AFRICA

The blond-haired young man and dog entered the Mayor's home in the middle of the night. He took a packet of soil from his clothing and emptied it on the kitchen and living room floors. The young man then went into the bathroom and wrote on the mirror in red lettering *DEATH TO EARTH.* He quietly left the home and walked the short distance to the city center. Along the way, he periodically dumped some of the remaining soil he had along the walkways. The massive dog followed obediently behind him, but careful not to put its paws on the dropped soil.

"The sun will be up soon and will work this soil into a poisonous vapor. No one will survive the day. The wind will take it throughout the city and life will cease to exist in Libreville." He looked down at the dog sitting beside him. A low growl escaped the animal and they continued to walk out of town.

When the sun rose into the sky, its heat reacted with the soil and whisks of vapor rose and extended itself throughout the area. People began falling to the ground all over the city. The Mayor had got up from his night's rest at mid-morning via the ringing of his cell phone by his bed. The person at the other end was hysterical and not making any sense from what the Mayor was hearing. He left his bedroom and walked into the living room and immediately felt sick. He looked down at his legs and saw that they were turning white in color. The last thing he remembered was seeing his feet disintegrate as he collapsed onto the floor.

By noontime, the City of Libreville was simply represented by its infrastructure. Mounds of soil were seen everywhere, both outside and within the buildings themselves. Not a sound was heard. The representation of Libreville, its people, ceased to exist.

RESISTANCE ATTACK AT AIRPORT

Hunter approached the wire with two other resistance personnel, lay silent for a full minute and the reached up and cut the fencing in three places. He was the first to slip through followed by the other two men. They approached the tall communications tower and one of the men began climbing up the side to the top some 40 feet up. He placed a explosive charge on either side of the tall antenna and quietly set the timer. The man climbed down and told Hunter that it would blow in five minutes.

 "Good work. Let's get over to that hangar and see if we can't create a little more havoc inside."

The side door was bolted shut. They started to around to the front when the hangar door started to swing open. A rebel sat at the wheel of a tow truck and began taking one of their fighters out to the tarmac. They remained motionless in the dim light and let the individual and aircraft go by before they entered the building. Inside, sat three fighters and a troop carrier aircraft. No one was around. Hunter told the two men to plant charges on the troop carrier while he set his on each of the three fighters. He told the men to start a three-minute countdown. When the bombs were set, they quickly exited the building and moved to a point where they initially cut the wire. In precisely five minutes after the tower charges were set, it exploded and collapsed to the ground below. Almost at the same time, the aircraft within the hangar blew up taking the roofing out at the same time.

Sirens sounded all over the base as the

rebel reaction force surfaced everywhere. The timing couldn't have been better. As personnel were attempting to scramble to get their aircraft in the air and others trying to put out the hangar fire, Shawn's Razor came in swiftly and raked the aircraft apron with withering fire. His cannon tore up several fighters before anyone could get them into the air. As he sped past and banked hard left, Christopher's Leopard followed with another volley of fire power as he too destroyed aircraft, one on a takeoff roll. Crawford came around again and found the munitions bunker and obliterated it with an air-to-ground missile. The area lit up with a tremendous explosion throwing shrapnel in all directions and cutting down personnel in the immediate area.

 Just as Shawn pulled his aircraft out of the area, Bob Gonzales timed his Cheyenne entry into the fight perfectly. He raked the fuel deport with withering Gatling gun fire that resulted in another explosion that lit up the sky. He mopped up with neutralizing any vehicles still remaining.

 As both aircraft exited the airspace over the airport, several resistance ground troops began picking off rebel fighters in the open. For good measure, Shawn and Christopher made subsequent runs with the aircraft resulting in the destruction of the remaining buildings.

Not a single shot was fired by the rebel base forces and they were taken completely by surprise. With the communications tower eliminated at the outset, radio traffic outside the base was nonexistent. It would be hours before anyone in the rebel hierarchy knew that their aircraft base existed no longer.

THE INTERNATIONAL SPACE STATION

The commander was awakened from a fitful sleep by the watch officer and told to come to the control room. He maneuvered his way through the narrow

'halls' and entered the control room.
"What have we got?" he asked.

 "Sir, we have a large force of what appears to be space ships approaching our sector very shortly. They are moving in a way that will bring them very close to Earth within the next few days. Those blips we had seen prior to today, well, they aren't inanimate objects like space clutter. They are too well organized. And, besides that, our far-reaching telescope identified a glint of uniform metal on the leading object. I know that this sounds incredible, but I think our Planet is about to be invaded!"

 The commander took a lot at the data and immediately telecommunicated with

Ground Control. Houston Control responded with an evacuation order for all space station personnel. Emergency craft for such use were to be prepped and used as quickly as possible. No one was to be left behind.

 "Houston, did you know that this fleet of ships were coming our way and, if so, why weren't we warned ahead of time?"

 "Commander, apparently Sydney Control Station conjectured that an armada from the Planet Kepler and led by a rogue leader was advancing on Earth as early as last week. We just found about it today when we intercepted rebel forces already positioned on Earth attempting to neutralize major cities around the world with a chemical/biological agent. Us the emergency protocol plan that was set up specifically for this reason. Get your people out of there immediately, Commander."

 Communications were then shut down and the Commander sounded an emergency alarm that was heard throughout the Space Station. Personnel scrambled to their stations to initiate a departure plan to be effective should such a situation occur. When all had completed their assigned responsibilities, the Commander was notified and the egress from the Station commenced.

Should one was able to see the Station with an ultra powerful scope from Earth, he would have seen small explosive lights that radiated out from the Station and into space. Within the hour, all escape modules were accounted for on Earth. Retrieval aircraft had monitored each capsule and was there to receive its personnel at the projected landing site.

RESISTANCE GROUP

Lynn telecommunicated with her higher headquarters and filed her report. They were pleased with her proactive mission to lessen the overall threat on Kepler. Indeed, it spurred their own effort to confront the rebel forces in other areas to the extent that there was no longer opposition to original government personnel. They employed her tactics and completed hit and run attacks in every area where there was a substantial possibility of retaliation. The Keplerians were getting back on their feet and soon in a position to handle the more immediate concern of their sun burning out.

 Shawn approached Joshua and told him that they were overstaying their welcome and said that they would be returning to Earth, the Good Entity willing. He also stressed that he would seek the highest authority worldwide to convince them to accept the Keplerian population before they met their end.

Joshua thanked all of them for everything they did for the Planet and its people and wished them well on their journey. He hoped that their delay in meeting once again would be short-lived and that a 'joyous reunion' with Earth would be forth-coming.

 Shawn got together with Christopher, Hunter and Bob to let them know that they were leaving. He outlined his plan and hoped The Entity was in concert with HIS own timing.

 Just before departing in the Leopard and Cheyenne, Joshua approached them at their aircraft and made Shawn an offer. Knowing all too well that Krixus was on Earth's doorstep, he told

Crawford that he was giving them two of their spaceships to take to Earth to assist in denying the threat. He was giving them the Razor and another ship that Shawn was unaware of at this point. It was called the Raptor. As he was listening to Joshua, a tow vehicle brought the Raptor over and unhooked it beside the Razor.

 Shawn was speechless! He had died and gone to Space Heaven! He walked quickly over to the new space ship and unlatched the hatch. He climbed in and sat in the Commander's chair. There were two pilot's stations to his front and to his left and right. He station had a set of master controls that would allowed him to fly the ship by himself. He gazed at the controls and quickly grasped the order to which they had been laid out. He jumped out of the seat and exited the aircraft. Shawn went over and gave Joshua a bear hug in gratitude. He did have some resulting questions or concerns.

 "Who flies the Razor? Is one of your people coming with us through the gateway?"

 "No, Father, I'll be driving the Razor," remarked Christopher with a wry grin. "You know that I'm a quick study when it comes to flying and noted carefully everything you did when we first went up in the Razor. I don't think you have anything to worry about." Crawford merely shook his head, looked at Hunter and Bob, and threw up his hands in defeat.

THE DIMENSIONAL GATEWAY

Shawn led the flight on takeoff in the Razor, followed by Bob and Hunter in the Cheyenne, and then Christopher in the Raptor. As the Cheyenne was the slowest aircraft in the flight of three, Shawn kept an eye on him so that he wouldn't lag too far behind. They climbed to 3,000 feet and leveled off. Five minutes later, a bluish tint of a cloud appeared at Shawn's eleven oçlock. He notified the others of his siting.

 Crawford didn't have to align the Raptor with the cloud; the cloud aligned itself with the three aircraft. One by one, they entered the bluish mist and remained in its grip for about 30 seconds. Prior to exiting, everyone heard the familiar voice of The Entity bellowing out a laugh that denied competition. "Shawn, Christopher, Hunter and Bob, it's so good to see you all in good spirits and well. My friends, the time is at hand when you must stop Krixus and his fleet of ships from entering the Earth's atmosphere. He will stop at nothing to dominate and cast his will upon everyone on the Planet. "I am always with you."

 They came out into clear skies and over land that Shawn immediately recognized as that of Houston, Texas. The controller at the space station annex was waiting for them when he said, "Flight of three entering Houston airspace, you are cleared to land Runway 29L. Winds 220-degrees at 15 knots. Altimeter is 30.04. Welcome home!"

 That voice sounded awfully familiar, thought Shawn. Almost as though he knew the individual personally. Then, another voice came over the intercom, this one a female who said, "Better get your butt down here immediately, Cowboy!" Now that voice he was very

The Raptor Spaceship

familiar with, so much so that the others in their aircraft just chuckled.

"Seems like old home week, Shawn,"remarked Bob Gonzales from his Cheyenne. "Mother!" Christopher added. And Hunter couldn't resist, "Bob, we should probably let Shawn land first or we will never hear the last of it from his Wife Christine."

"Father, you know that we all love you. I'll protect you from this ragged group of vagabonds," his Daughter Colette chipped in over the radio.

Crawford, just shook his head in wonder. I can't go anywhere without Christine knowing about where I've gone. Before landing instructions were given, Shawn quipped, "Anyone ready for some Pizza?"

 Once on the ground and out of their aircraft, the reunion was something very special. Christine hugged everyone, especially her Son Christopher. "Did he behave while you two were out wandering the cosmos, Christopher?"

 "Mother, I had my hands full with him. Glad I was there to keep him out of trouble." Shawn looked at him with one raised eyebrow and said, "No Pizza for you!!"

 Commander Morrison and her Husband Vice Commander O'Leary came over and gave them all a hug. They had been waiting for the immediate family to get

together for the welcome home greeting.
Shawn looked at O'Leary for a second
and said, "Was that you giving landing
instructions prior to our arrival?"

 "The one and the same," said O'Leary.
Thought you would need a familiar
voice after being off the Planet' for
awhile. It's good to see you, Shawn.
We have a lot to talk about. Allison,"
he said to his wife, "Why don't we get
started on the debriefing with everyone.
We don't have much time."

 Shawn got everyone together and they
all went into the space station terminal
and into its spacious conference room.
Commander Morrison was the first to
speak and told all that she was happy to

have them 'home' again. She turned it over to her Husband Vice Commander Michael O'Leary who echoed her sentiment about their safe return.

 "Shawn, Dr. Canastra's belief in an imminent invasion from the Planet Kepler was right on. The Space Station personnel evacuated this morning when they confirmed that the invading armada was on our doorstep. They were all recovered safely. Two hours later, the lead ship of the approaching force blew the Station to bits. I think the leader, Krixus, I believe is his name, thought that having the Space Station viable was crucial to our defense. With you here and your two spaceships, we have a fighting chance of turning back the rebels, and, even defeating them."

Shawn looked at O'Leary, a Friend he had been through multiple gateways with over the years, and said, "Sir, we have only two spacecraft. This is certainly not enough to defeat the many ships heading our way."

Christopher looked at Colette who smiled broadly. "Father," she said, "We have those who will never forget what you've done on Planet Kepler. They, in turn, will not let us down. Father, look to the east for a moment. You'll see a familiar bluish cloud develop. Out of that cloud will emerge hundreds of Keplerian resistance fighters who will insure that Krixus never sets foot on this

Planet."

Seconds later, the first of the fighters came out of the cloud, followed by another and another. Soon the sky was filled with Keplerian spaceships all arranged perfectly in sequential rows and hovering at 1000 feet. One of the lead ships flashed its external light down toward those watching.

"Father, Joshua and his Mother Lynn have come to insure that our freedom will never be in jeopardy ever again."

There was just enough room for all spaceships to land at the huge airfield. Their arrival created a huge interest, needless to say, as base personnel emptied out of the buildings and vehicular traffic on the adjacent highways came to a stand still.

 From the lead space shift that settled 50 meters away from Shawn and his group, came Lynn followed by her Son Joshua. When they reached the group, Lynn introduced herself and her Son to the others. The only thing that she said was, "Tell us what to do."

KRIXUS ARMADA

After taking out the Space Station with a tremendous bolt of laser energy, Krixus brought his armada to a standstill in space and overlooking North America. He told his communications officer to initiate a call to the Rebel ground forces to initiate their subversive activities. He would wait 48 hours for those below on Earth to complete their mission that would surely cripple the leadership ability to react to his invasion. Or so he thought.

He brought his armada in a horizontal line above the Earth. He directed his Spaceship Commanders to deflect their arrival to their assigned major city and to be prepared on order to fire their weapons at each capitol building on earth. There was to be unimaginable devastation.

HOUSTON COMMAND CENTER

The frequencies used by Krixus and his fleet were known to Joshua and Lynn. Even though their communications were somewhat more advanced, Joshua was able to get with experts there in Houston and manipulate receivers to access the rebel transmissions. It didn't take long for all on the ground to realize that Krixus' intent was to spread out his forces all over the Planet and that they had less than 48 hours to effect a course of action that would defeat their plan.

Shawn, Christopher and Joshua

developed an outline of attack on Krixus and each of his spaceships prior to their unleashing their might on central Earth cities. Within 24 hours, Keplerian ships fanned out surreptitiously all over the globe, at each major city, and waited for the order to attack the enemy fleet. Shawn was to lead a group of six Keplerian fighters in the Raptor. Christopher would be his wing man and assist in protecting his flank and six oçlock position by flying the Razor.

 They would not wait for the order given by Krixus to commence the attack, but would take the initiative at each location and destroy the rebel ships before they could fire a shot. Of course, this appeared to be a simultaneous

counterattack by the Keplerian fighters
for none of Krixus spaceships would fire
without his express order to negotiate
their targets.

Shawn would lead the attack on Krixus
main battle spaceship with Christopher
on his wing. The timing of neutralizing
the rebel attack was critical. Too soon a
push would alert Krixus that could
easily sway the result of the battle.

In Shawn's cockpit sat a device that
showed each of the Keplerian fighters
around the globe. When each fighter
was in position and they had its target in
sight, they would initiate their ambush
of the enemy vessel by taking the most
advantageous angle for a shot at the

most vulnerable area of the rebel hull. Each would continue to fire his pulse weapons until the rebel spaceship fell to the Earth. If thee were survivors, they would be taken prisoner and handed over eventually to Lynn and her leadership.

 One by one a blip representing a Keplerian fighter shone solidly on Shawn's screen. With one hour to go before Krixus would unleash his spaceships upon Earth's leadership, the last blip lit up on the monitor.

 Crawford gave the "go"code to all Keplerians to take out their designated targets. At the same time, he and Christopher launched their spacecraft in the direction of Krixus command vessel. They approached within five kilometers and took the pulse shot at the most vulnerable area.

Krixus was alerted to the attack from Earth by his science officer. He immediately went into a defensive mode in an effort to withstand the initial volley against his spaceship. His best course of action would have been to fire before being fired upon, but the attack from Earth caught him completely by surprise. How did they acquire these advanced spaceships, he wondered. His hesitation caused him to delay just enough for Shawn to punch a laser-like hole in the rebel's hull.

Krixus returned fire and one of his shots hit Shawn and crippled his fighter. His direction of flight was directly at the enemy vessel. He had no control over his handling of the Raptor and was heading straight toward Krixus at an amazing speed. This isn't to end well he said to himself.

At the last moment, a side door to his immediate front opened and out flew a rebel fighter. It banked hard to the right and missed seeing Shawn's advance to the command ship. Hard to believe, but his spaceship was aligned perfectly with the outer door that showed a flat landing area just inside the ship. He manipulated his thrusters to slow the Raptor down as much as possible, but he was still coming in fast.

 The Raptor nearly and completely by-
passed a side wall. A winglet was torn
off to his left and he skidded sideways
on the flat deck within the ship. His
forward progress was slowed but not
nearly enough before he hit the back
wall with a tremendous jolt. The bay
door behind him closed.

 He was dazed for a moment, but
quickly reacted quickly enough to look
around him. He felt his ears pop as
pressure was reinstated within the area.
No one else was in that bay. He got out
of the Raptor and hid behind some
materiel stored on the floor. He waited
for a full minute for any sounds or

voices and then proceeded to walk along the wall until he came to a ladder. He looked both ways before climbint to the top where he found an unlocked door. He went through and came face to face with the largest rebel he was ever going to see. Crawford's black belt training instinctively kicked in and he thrust his fingers into the man's throat. The rebel went down with both hands holding below his chin as his eyes rolled back into head.

 He didn't stick around. Shawn left the room and entered a long hallway. Two men came out of one of the rooms just as Crawford passed by. As they were surprised to see him aboard the spacecraft, they both hesitated before taking action of their own. But this was too late.

 Shawn drop kicked one of the men in the groin, quickly turned 360-degrees and swept his leg around to catch the second man in the calf area. They both went down and Crawford finished them off by striking each individual with his fist on the bridge of the nose, thereby collapsing the cartilage into the brain. They died immediately.

 He came to another ladder that led up to walkway and took it to the top. As he passed one of the closed rooms, he heard a man say, "Commander, we are severely damaged. Do you wish to give the order to abandon the ship?"

"No, you fool," another voice answered. This was followed by a blast from a weapon and Shawn heard a man collapse against a bulkhead and fall to the floor. Crawford looked through a crack in the doorway and saw one man hovering over a computer system while he held the fired weapon still in his hand. His back was to Shawn and the latter sensed no one else in the room. He opened the door and approached the man whose back was still hunched over a radar scope. Krixus felt his presence and immediately turned around and pointed his weapon at Shawn. His only defense was to bring his leg up straight and into the man's hand. The weapon went flying to the side. Krixus charged

Crawford who side stepped him and pushed him forward into a side wall. The rebel hit his head against the metal and was dazed for a second. He charged Shawn again. This time Crawford took his full weight to the side and threw him over his back where he lay unconscious. Krixus didn't move and wasn't breathing. Shawn knelt down beside him and felt for a pulse. There was none.

 He got up and looked around the control room. He saw communications equipment to the front and went over to it. He hit a switch and immediately heard radio traffic, Keplerian radio traffic. In the mix, he heard Christopher broadcasting something about his Father was aboard Krixus battle spaceship. He also said that the warship was beginning to disintegrate from all of the pulse hits it took from the Keplerian fighters.

 Shawn then said into the communications array, "Christopher, is that you out there?"

 Immediately, his Son came back and said, "Father, is that you? Where are you aboard the ship?"

 "In the command center. Krixus has been incapacitated and I'm looking for an Uber to come by and pick me up. I tip pretty well. Are you available at the moment?"

 "Father, there is an open bay door

middle of the spaceship. It's clear for me to put the Razor through without damage. Do you have a breathing apparatus nearby?"

 Crawford looked around and saw a spacesuit attached to the wall to the rear of the room. "I have one. Let me meet you downstairs. It should take me five minutes to get amidship. What do you like on your Pizza?"

 He left hurriedly and went down two ladders before he came to what he believed was the middle of the ship. All of a sudden close by, he heard the screeching of metal as if something huge had just slid across the flooring. He donned his breathing apparatus and opened a side door. There, sitting comfortably and smiling from ear to ear was his Son Christopher. He had an oxygen mask on and opened the hatch door. Shawn climbed into the co-pilot seat and bent over to hug his Son.

 "Now, how do we get out of here, young man?"

 "Father, I've had a bit of practice maneuvering this spaceship. Watch and wonder."

 Christopher manipulated the thrusters and turned the ship around 180-degrees. The metal to metal screeching was almost too much to bear. Once lined up with the open door, he added power to the spacecraft and they began to move forward. Just before reaching the opening and out into space, Crawford heard a loud rumbling sound off to his right. As soon as they cleared the spaceship's door and out into space, Krixus ship began exploding from rear to front. They had just escaped a catastrophic explosion. Space debris shot everywhere about them. Fortunately, the Razor withstood any of the hits and the spaceship headed toward Earth and the Houston Space complex.

HOUSTON SPACE CENTER

Christopher was the first to exit the

Razor and was met by his Mother Christine who wrapped her arms around him and held him for a long moment. Shawn waltzed over as though he had just taken a walk around the complex ans said, "Hey, all. Did anyone miss me?"

 They all turned their backs on him and took two steps forward. They then turned around and charged him slapping him on the back and congratulating him for his heroics aboard Krixus spaceship. Lynn and Joshua stood off to the side and took in Shawn's false bravado as he exaggerated his entire role in Krixus' demise. She then approached him and gave him a big hug and kiss on the cheek. She then turned to Christine and said, "Don't ever lose this one. He's very special."

 Crawford blushed, recovered and invited everyone to Houston's mess that was adorned like 5-star restaurant. He told everyone that the Coach was buying and not to hold back on their orders. Hunter looked at Shawn and said to everyone, "Great, I've got Shawn's credit card. Let's go have some fun."

SPECIAL UNITED NATIONS SESSION

Two weeks later, in New York, Shawn,

Lynn, Joshua and Christopher appeared before the general assembly of the United Nations. As he was introduced by a prominent scientist whose field was in extraterrestrial planetary travel and who was well respected in his field, Shawn gathered his notes and proceeded to the podium. When he reached the center of the room, he looked at every member of the Council for a brief moment and then said, "I would like for my Son, Christopher, Joshua and Lady Lynn to join me."

"Distinguished Ladies and Gentlemen," he began. "Thousands of years ago, Planet Earth was inhabited by a species of people much more advanced than ourselves presently. You may have heard of their home: Atlantis. Lady Lynn and her Son Joshua represent the heritage of those marvelous people whose real home was but a space shuttle away from Planet Earth. You see, Planet Kepler was a Sister Planet whose advancement in science took precedence over that of Earth's desire to excel in Commerce. They lived on our world in that fabled city off of the African Coast and in the Atlantic Ocean. Their feats of accomplishment are even seen today in the Pyramids, for example. Their representation on Easter Island, in my mind, doesn't do them justice, but they were honored for their contributions to Earth's well-being while they existed and beyond their time here on Earth.

"Their Planet's sun is dying. I come before you today to accept the Keplerian people here on Earth before their people are gone forever. We have the wherewithal to take these advanced, wonderful and scientifically experienced people right now. Their transfer to Earth will be seamless and thorough. With their inclusion here on our Planet, we will be able to reap the benefit of their scientific knowledge and, as incredible as it may sound, even get to know one another here on Earth better through the sharing of new ideas and innovative ways of thinking. This is more than a humanitarian effort; it is a gesture of moral conviction that we, on this Planet, are much better than what we think we are. All we have to do is look inward and see the true goodness in each and every one of us."

THE KEPLERIAN INCLUSION

It was a unanimous vote by all members of the United Nations community to proceed with inclusion of the Keplerian people into our world. The transition was remarkable to watch as their scientific community rose beyond all measure to make the physical transference as smooth as possible.

Fourteen months following the exodus

from Kepler, their sun died out. One
can only wonder what it would have
been like to perish in a frozen wasteland
if the Earth had not stepped up in the
belief of the goodness of mankind.

GABON, WEST AFRICA

The blond haired young man sat on a
rock near the crater. His massive hound
sat nearby looking up at him. He looked
around him and saw nothing viable, not
a living creature existed. The young
man smiled and thought that the work
that he had done here would one day
prove to be the downfall of Planet Earth.

Libreville and its surrounding area was considered a "no-man's land". It was another Chernobyl of sorts, only much more deadly. Soon they would come to attempt to clear the region of this threat to all humanity and they will then experience suffering like never before. He smiled and then laughed loudly at the possibilities.

AUTHOR BIOGRAPHY

Timothy James LTC O'Leary, III is a retired U.S. Army Lieutenant Colonel with 27 years of active duty and reserve service to his Country. Tim served a tour of duty in both Vietnam and the First Persian Gulf Wars. He is a graduate of the Defense Language Institute in Monterey, California where he earned a diploma in Italian Language training. Tim is a helicopter pilot with 2,200 hours of flight time in UH-1 and OH-58 aircraft with the United States Army. During Operation Desert Storm, Tim was a medevac pilot with the 217th Medical Battalion. His final tour of duty was Battalion Commander of the 286th Supply and Service Battalion.

He has a B.A. degree in Sociology and French, and holds a Master of

Education and Educational Specialist degrees in Educational Administration and Supervision from Georgia Southern College. Tim was a Doctor of Education degree candidate at the University of Virginia in Educational Administration and Supervision. He also has one year of

Spanish Language training at the University of Southern Maine in Portland. Tim taught foreign language and social studies in the Georgia public school system for three years and was an assistant principal at a secondary education school in Virginia. Tim has run 13 marathons to include the Marine

Corps in 1994 and Boston's 100th in 1996. He has been a baseball umpire for over 40 years and has officiated five Cal Ripken World Series. Tim was selected to umpire the Africa/European Little League Regional in The Netherlands in July 2020. He has also umpired three Eastern Regional Junior Softball Tournaments for Little League Headquarters. He currently serves on the Maine Little League District 6 Board as a Liaison Coordinator for the District Administrator. Tim played varsity baseball at Georgia Southern, semi-professional ball in Italy, and did a baseball tour with the European Continental Cavaliers Team in South Africa in 1971. Tim has three children

and five grandchildren. He and his Wife
Lynn reside in Gorham, Maine.